Don·t Cry
for LOVE

SHAR STURGES

KP PUBLISHING COMPANY

ISBN: 978-1-950936-98-4 (Paperback)
ISBN: 978-1-950936-23-6 (Ebook)
Library of Congress Control Number: Pending

Editor: KP Publishing Services
Cover Design: Juan Roberts, Creative Lunacy
Interior Design: Jennifer Houle
Literary Director: Sandra Slayton James

Published by:

KP Publishing Company
Publisher of Fiction, Nonfiction & Children's Books
Valencia, CA 91355
www.kp-pub.com

Printed in the United States of America

ACKNOWLEDGMENTS

I thank God for giving me such a delightful gift of writing. To my husband Durron, thank you and I love you.

Thank you to my grandparents, especially my great-grandparents (RIP), grandfathers (RIP), grandmothers (Mother—*RIP* and Grandmommy), parents (Phillip, Rene and Mom Emerson), brothers (Jermain, Jeremy and Jerahn—you can do anything you want), my uncles, aunts, cousins, my sister's in Christ—wouldn't have made without your prayers.

To my in-laws: Stanley (Pops)—*RIP*, Mama Tee, Mama Pinkey, brothers-in-law, sisters-in-law, uncles, cousins, nieces, nephews—(too many in-laws to name), family friends, true friends, and co-workers, thank you for the support.

Thank you Pastor Richard Williams III and First Lady Laverne, for support and direction, and thank you to the Victory family (hey, hey holla).

Thank you Rev. Richardson, Sis. Richardson (RIP), and church family. Mama Simone thank you for adopting me as your daughter.

Thank you everyone who purchased this book, it could not be a success without you. God bless you!

We finally did it Uncle Mike and Auntie Gail! LOL!
AGAIN!!!

CHAPTER ONE

was not ready to go to Randy's funeral service. I pulled the covers back and stared at the glossy painted ceiling in my apartment. Attending the funeral service would be a bittersweet reunion. As callous as those words sounded, it was true.

I stepped into my house shoes and walked slowly to the shower. It seemed farther away than any other day. Suddenly, I lost my balance. I felt light-headed, nauseated, and groggy. There was a sharp pain in my stomach. I fell halfway to the floor. The pain throbbed and jolted, as if someone tugged my insides. I sat Indian style on the floor. I rocked back and forth and held my breath. Was God trying to tell me something? Well, if He were, did I ever listen? I continued my journey to the shower. I ran the hot water and whimpered.

I dropped my robe to the floor and opened the shower door. A quick flash of Randy gathered in my mind. I heard Randy's disembodied voice:

"Hey baby. Come and join me for a hot shower."

"Randy, I don't have time. I have to go to your funeral."

"Come on. I won't try anything. I promise," he said with a smooth tongue.

The phone rang. Startled, I jumped out of the shower, grabbed my robe, and ran to the living room.

"You have a collect call from Blythe Penitentiary."

I immediately pressed the button to connect the call.

"Hey baby girl."

"Hey dad."

"Are you going to Randy's funeral today?"

"Yeah."

"I don't know why. He never treated you like you were meant to be treated."

"I know dad, but I'm going."

"All right, I'll check on you later."

Without notice, I heard a click and then a dial tone. My dad never said goodbye. He felt goodbyes were bad luck. I guess our last name should be the "Badlucks" instead of the Summers. Bad Luck Chuck was my dad's street name. People always said that when my dad came to see you, it was bad luck. I knew my dad's history, but I didn't want it to know me.

I was afraid to go back to the shower for fear Randy would haunt me. Despite my reservations, I went back. The water was cold. I turned the nozzle over to extreme hot. Randy kissed my neck.

"Why did you do it? Why did you do it, Beauty?"

I whimpered, gasping for air. I quickly rubbed my body down with Victoria's Secret shower gel. What secret did Victoria know and how long would it be before she told? After the water failed to get any hotter, I rinsed the soap off, attempting to wash my aches and pains down the drain.

The funeral service started at 10:00 a.m. I left home and took the surface streets to the mortuary. The moment I arrived, I saw Randy's mom exiting the limo. Ms. Henderson wanted me to ride with the family, but I felt much better in my own solitude. I sat in my car for several minutes. Once I saw Ms. Henderson enter the building, I proceeded to walk in without removing my sunglasses. I was too afraid to show my red, watery eyes. My heart shattered into pieces like a new puzzle scattered in a box. I loved Randy more than anything in the world. At some point, I knew he would settle down. I had no idea it would be in a dark grey casket. I felt completely empty. Randy's mother sat moribund on the front pew next to Natalie, Randy's sister. I contemplated how many women Randy slept with were there. Yes, Randy was brutal. He was a womanizer, and he simply did not care, but for one reason or another, I loved him.

I grabbed my stomach. The pain was back. I held my breath in hopes the discomfort went away. I continued to breathe slowly until the soreness subsided. I held the obituary and noticed the picture on the front. I remembered when Randy took it. In fact, I picked out the shirt he wore. Tears welled in my eyes. I folded the obituary and put it in my purse.

The service had progressed. It was time for a solo. I saw Aunt Elizabeth. I sighed as she gracefully walked toward the front of the church in her tilted feather hat. Aunt Elizabeth was short and petite. Everyone in Randy's family respected her. Aunt Elizabeth did not have any children and was married six times. Her last husband left her for a younger woman. Randy used to say she killed her husbands. I knew one thing: she gave good advice on life. I loved to converse with Aunt Elizabeth. She listened to my poems while I recited them. She tried to help me conquer my fear of stage fright.

Aunt Elizabeth approached the front of the mortuary. She removed the cordless microphone from the stand. I never heard the song before; it was something about His eye on a sparrow. Aunt Elizabeth sounded beautiful. Her voice echoed like the sounds of Billie Holiday. Aunt Elizabeth's up and down octaves made the hair on my back stand at attention. When she finished her last verse, everyone cried, including me.

The minister spoke, "Thank you for that lovely solo. Now we will have one more selection by the choir, and then Reverend Towne will give the eulogy. After that, there will be the viewing of the body."

Halfway through the choir's song, Randy's mother wailed. She fainted and hit her head on the wooden bench. Randy's sister and the ushers escorted her out of the mortuary. The woman leading the song sounded horrible compared to Aunt Elizabeth. I wanted to grab the microphone myself. Quickly, Aunt Elizabeth walked to the choir stand and snatched the microphone. The choir continued to sing. No one reacted to Aunt Elizabeth's stunt. Once the choir and Aunt Elizabeth finished the song, she handed the microphone back to the woman and smiled. Classic.

"Uh, thank you Sister Lady for assisting the choir, and thank you Sister Johnson for allowing our guest to participate in a glorious fellowship," another minister said as he wiped the sweat cascading from his forehead.

Sister Johnson leaped to her feet and ran out the side door. It was time for the eulogy. Quietness fell upon the audience as if we all waited for a sign from God.

"To the beloved family and friends: Today marks a regrettable day, as God has decided to take back one of His own."

Did he just say one of God's own? God gave Randy over to Satan a long time ago.

"No one knows the time or day when we will cease from living, but I say to you all, learn of God and who He is," the minister said.

The minister turned to the family and said, "I know Randy was very dear. He was the epitome of compassion."

He definitely has the wrong Randy. Did Ms. Henderson pay the minister to say those remarks?

The minister continued, "I remember when I would see Randy. He always helped his mother out the car and smiled as he entered the church. The last time we spoke he said he was ready for God's great plan."

I must be at the wrong funeral!

"I want the family and friends to know, Randy is in a better place. Don't be sad, for Randy is smiling on us right now. Do not let your hearts be troubled. Trust in God. Please be strong, family. We will get an opportunity to see Randy again," the minister said.

I needed to excuse myself. Outside, the motorcycle escorts placed big yellow funeral stickers on all the cars. I asked one of the men if he knew where the restroom was. He pointed to another door adjacent to the mortuary.

The navy blue carpet and red painted walls created a somber hallway. The first room I passed had an open casket. There was an older man lying inside the casket with his arms folded across his chest. His shirt was stiffer than his body. He had grey hair and gold rings on every finger. His black suit accentuated the black and white interior of the casket. I whisked past the door, trying not to regurgitate. I finally noticed a sign that read "restroom." I ran and almost didn't make it to the toilet before my food gave way.

I went back into the mortuary to bid my Randy adieu. The minister was near the end of the eulogy. Ushers escorted Randy's mother and sister back inside the mortuary. The minister made it seem like Randy was a faithful churchgoer. Randy did not attend church unless his mother or sister asked him to come. He asked me to attend a few times, but the church thing was not for me. I didn't understand what all the hype was about church. In the news, there were stories about priests molesting children, ministers stealing the church's money, and preachers cheating on their wives. No thank you, I have enough drama in my life.

After the minister sat in his chair, the pallbearers walked toward the casket and pulled back the lid. Seeing Randy's handsome face revealed made mountainous tears fall from my eyes. My heart died with Randy. I had one last look at the man whom I loved and hated.

I walked down the aisle and faced his mother. I didn't look at his sister. I leaned down and gave Ms. Henderson a hug. I made my way toward the casket. How could he just lie there with a smile on his face, as if he were the perfect gentleman? Every wrong thing Randy ever did flashed in my mind. Angrily, I stuck out my middle finger. When I looked back, it looked like he gave me the middle finger too.

CHAPTER TWO

The sun was beaming. On the way to my car, Randy's sister ran toward me.

"Beauty! How do you have the audacity to show your face here?"

Natalie used to be my best friend. I met her in junior high. Natalie was a bit taller than me, and people used to think we were sisters. We were like twins, practically inseparable. We took the same classes together in high school and hung out on the weekends. I didn't pay her brother any attention back then because he was very irritating. Randy would tease and mimic our conversations. He dressed funny. I'd never thought we would be together today. Natalie and I lost touch when we went to different colleges out of state. After graduation, we moved back to L.A. and became two peas in a pod again. That's when my feelings for Randy deepened.

Our chemistry was strong. We became a couple and moved in together. Natalie was jealous. Natalie and I soon faded into a "hi and bye" relationship.

Randy was my everything. I couldn't believe how hard I fell for him. He complimented me every day and cooked breakfast for me Saturday mornings. Somehow I didn't see the true person he really was until it was too hard to let go. We practically did everything together. People didn't understand our relationship. It seemed, perfect - I thought.

It wasn't until a year later when the lies started to surface. I noticed he would stay out late. He began to lie about where he was or what he was doing. I remember one day Candice, an old friend, called me.

"Beauty, I'm here eating lunch at Red Lobster and I think I see Randy here with another woman," she said.

"Maybe that's his cousin. He said she was in town visiting and he was taking her out."

"I don't know about that. Do you want me to go over there and say something?" Candice asked.

"Definitely not. I don't want him thinking I sent you to spy on him. I trust Randy."

"Yeah, well at least somebody does, because from the looks of it, he's not worth being trusted. I think you should come meet me here," she said.

"No way!"

I stopped talking to Candice because she always tried to get me to break up with Randy. Had I known then what I knew now, I would've gone to Red Lobster and ended everything. I would have called the relationship off that very moment. I would've thanked Candice rather than push her to the side. I would've saved myself a lot of heartache and pain. Only if . . .

I forgot Natalie had asked me a question. I came back to reality.

"What do you mean what am I doing here?"

I was not in the mood to hear whatever Natalie had to say.

"You killed Randy!" She exclaimed.

I lost control, balled my fists, and hit her with all my might. She fell and her eyes fluttered. No one noticed she was on the ground, so I hurriedly left the scene.

I didn't plan on going to the gravesite. I was emotionally drained. I decided to go home and rest. I contemplated on how my life was changing, now that Randy was gone. I felt hopeless. I pulled into the parking stall and turned the ignition off. I was paralyzed with sadness. I leaned on the steering wheel and cried. Randy treated me wrong, but I couldn't control my pain. A part of me wished he was with me, and part of me was relieved I didn't have to deal with his lies. I wouldn't have to worry about when he was coming home or who he was with. I felt like peace should've been on my side, but it was nowhere in sight.

I managed to open the car door. My body felt weak. I dropped my keys on the ground. I stared at the keys and cried again. Sniffling, I got out the car, closed the door, and picked up the keys. I took the elevator to my floor. I didn't smile at the couple that held hands in the elevator. I stared with envy as they walked off, adoring each other's love. The elevator door closed and I went up one level. The elevator door opened. I walked to my apartment and stuck the key in the door. When I opened the door, I froze. I felt like Randy was sitting on the sofa, staring at me, asking me why was I sad. Then I realized he wasn't there. I closed the door and walked to the bedroom. I fell on the bed and cried again. I cried myself to sleep. That day was just the beginning of what I thought would be the end.

CHAPTER THREE

I can't take the pain of being lonely
I don't know how to love again
Sick and tired of these phonies
Like Toni Braxton, wishing I could breathe again
I'm not going to let you take my joy
I'm not going to give you that pleasure
I'm glad that you are gone
Ha ha ha, I hope you enjoy the hot weather

Writing poetry made my life livable. I, along with other poets, hung out at Joi's Café. The popular coffee house in West Los Angeles was a place where upcoming poets displayed their talents. One day I planned to get on stage and recite my poem, but I lacked courage. Aunt Elizabeth said my fear was only what I thought would happen if I failed. No matter how much she tried to encourage me, I couldn't get on stage. Randy never went with me to Joi's—my pleasure, his pain.

I sat in my car in the parking lot at Joi's. I couldn't focus. It was only a few days since I attended Randy's funeral. My heart still felt heavy. I cried when I saw couples kissing. I cried when I saw anything that remotely reminded me of Randy, from the car he drove to the cologne he wore. I was miserable and I didn't know how to cure the pain. I decided not to go inside and went for a drive. I ended up at Dockweiler Beach. I didn't get out the car, but rather sat in the car and stared at the ocean. The moonlight danced on the waves as my heart pounded with sorrow. My cell phone rang. It was Natalie. I didn't answer. I didn't want to hear anything she had to say. I let the call roll over to voicemail. My phone made another sound. Natalie sent me a text that read:

"Don't ever come around my family. You killed my brother and you will get what's coming!"

I couldn't believe this was the same Natalie who was my best friend. I didn't kill Randy. I had no idea why she kept insisting on why his death was my fault. I deleted her text message. I wasn't afraid of Natalie one bit. She was the least of my worries. I leaned my car seat back and closed my eyes.

"You sure know how to make a man feel good," Randy said as I massaged his back.

"I don't know what I'd do without you," I said.

Randy turned around and grabbed me by the waist. He kissed me like I was his one and only. It was Friday night, and we didn't have any plans. We spent a romantic evening at home until Randy's cell phone rang. He picked up the phone and started talking as he walked toward the bedroom. A few minutes later, he told me that his sister called him crying, because she broke up with her boyfriend and she wanted him to come over. Immediately the mood changed. I didn't buy his story. I couldn't call Natalie because our relationship was severed.

"I thought we were spending a romantic evening together."

"We will pick up when I get back. I'll be over there for an hour or two. I'll call you when I get there," Randy said.

He grabbed his coat and keys and kissed me on my lips. Just like that. He was gone. He didn't come home until the next afternoon.

I woke up remembering I was in my car. The waves had subsided to subtle ripples against the sand. The excruciating pain in my stomach was back. I sat still with my hands over my stomach. I crunched over in pain. A few minutes later the cramping stopped. I decided to call it night and head back home. I felt lonely and didn't know what to do with my life.

When I arrived home I went straight to bed. I pulled back the covers halfway and laid in a fetal position. The sheets were cold. My pillow was flat and I couldn't get comfortable. I tossed and turned until I finally fell asleep.

CHAPTER FOUR

sat on the sofa and turned on the television. Before I could relax, I heard a woman's loud voice.

"You better stay away from my man! I'm sick and tired of you showing up here. You don't know me, and you don't want to know me! Now come closer and you will!"

I could tell it was my neighbor Sarai from her high-pitched voice. She has the most handsome husband on Earth. Last year, I saw Sarai's husband Doug for the first time, standing outside the apartment building. I never told Randy or Sarai that's how I noticed the "For Lease" sign. I couldn't keep my eyes off his bulging muscles.

"Hi, beautiful," Doug said charismatically.

"Hi." I leaned slightly to my right to read the "For Lease" sign again.

"Do you know if any apartments are still available?" I couldn't think of anything else to say.

"If it is, I hope to share it with you," he said.

I laughed nervously. He was extremely tall. I later found out that he played international basketball. He had a deep, dark complexion with a short fade and a shapely goatee. He wore black and red basketball shorts with a red T-shirt. His tennis shoes were immaculately clean. His deeply defined calves caught my attention as his chest protruded through his sleeveless shirt. My thoughts alone would have perturbed Randy.

When I came back to reality, I noticed the titanium band on his left ring finger. I continued to stare. I walked up a few stairs and pulled a brochure from a clear box.

I never told Sarai about our conversation and I definitely didn't tell her what happened when I moved in.

"Sarai, are you OK?"

"Of course! Doug's sorry, baby wannabe mama is here, and it's about to be a problem!"

She yelled as the other woman briskly walked away.

"I am so sick and tired of her coming here begging for money! I'm going to give her something to really beg for if she keeps at it."

I tried to defuse the situation.

"I'm going to Joi's tonight. Do you want to go?"

"Sure. I need to talk to you about something anyway."

"All right. I'll come over in about an hour."

I didn't give a second thought as to what Sarai wanted to talk about. Lately, all I could think about was Randy. It's been a month since Randy's death. Destined to have a good time tonight despite my feelings of depression, I walked to my closet and pulled back the shutters. Last week, I noticed my clothes were squeezed to one side of the closet, even though Aunt Elizabeth came and took all of Randy's belongings. I noticed a shirt of Randy's I wore from time to time balled up on the floor. I picked it up. I could smell his cologne. I still could not come to terms that Randy was gone for good. He could sell me the world repeatedly; take the same piece, jazz it up, and present it to me a different way. Little did he know that I learned his game better than he taught it to himself.

At the beginning of our relationship, everything was great. Our first date made me feel like Randy was the man of my dreams.

"Where do you want to go eat?" Randy asked as he drove behind the wheel of his red convertible Mustang.

"I don't know. Anywhere will be fine."

"Anywhere?"

"Yes. I trust your judgment."

He took me to some fancy restaurant in Malibu. We talked about our childhood, what our dreams were, and things we had in common. Randy was suave. He knew exactly what to say, how to say it, even if it weren't true. Every part of me wanted to spend all my time with him. Had I known our relationship would turn into four years of empathic hurt, I would've ended our friendship that night. Instead, I let my heart lead the way to destruction. I knew from that night forward we would be together forever. I had no idea it would be his forever.

CHAPTER FIVE

The ride to Joi's was pleasant. Sarai made me forget about my feelings of depression. She plugged in her iPod. We reminisced over songs we listened to growing up.

"Uh! Uh! Remember this one?" Sarai asked.

Sarai sung the lyrics to *"I Need Love"* by LL Cool J. I chimed in. We knew every word from the beginning to the end. We giggled and teased each other like two mischievous high school girls. We parked across the street from Joi's. There were many people entering the building because of the poet contest. Luckily, Joi kept my name on the guest list. I never had to wait in line. Envious eyes from women and drooling men followed Sarai's every move. Sarai was a personal trainer to several celebrities, and had the body to make her own mama resentful. We walked into Joi's and took a seat at my favorite table. Nikki, the weekend server, walked over and started writing on the tablet.

"I know Beauty wants the 'usual'," Nikki said.

"Sarai, what do you want to drink? I'm buying," I said.

"I'll have a Long Island iced tea. That'll last me all night," Sarai said.

We all laughed as I told Sarai we might need to call a cab to take us home tonight.

"All right, a Watermelon Daiquiri for Beauty, and a Long Island iced tea for you," Nikki said, pointing the top of her pen toward Sarai.

Nikki was very amicable. She always wore a smile on her face even when people were belligerent after a few drinks.

"I'll be right back with your drinks," Nikki said.

While we waited on Nikki to return, Cyfin, a usual performer, took the stage. Her hair was naturally curly. She wore a white top with flowers on it and light blue jeans. The flower in her hair complemented her glowing skin. Many people felt Cyfin favored Jill Scott, an R&B singer.

The D.J. played a soft mellow jazz tune.

"How y'all doin' out there tonight?" Cyfin asked.

"We're doing fine, just how you look," a man shouted from the audience.

"Oh my, well, thank you. I'm going to recite for y'all tonight, *Life*."

Cyfin closed her eyes and swayed from side to side in rhythm with the music. Her vocals echoed through the speakers.

> "You know, sometimes we get ourselves
> Into positions unknown to fate
> I mean we can't even relax
> Sit or even just wait
> We're made to love ourselves
> Deep, deep
> So deep
> That sometimes we can't help but weep
>
> Have you ever looked at the moon
> For all it's worth?
> I mean, damn
> Its beauty
> Its fullness surrounding Mother Earth

DON'T CRY FOR LOVE

The moon . . .
And, sometimes it stares right at me
Fooling me
Having me feeling down and out, lonely, and blue

Don't be dismayed
When the love starts to fade
Away from you
Into this big black ocean of love
Sometimes you have to stay and breathe
You feel that
Yeah! Breathe. Um, Um, Um, Um
Yeah
Love is a funny thing
Sometimes you feel it
Sometimes you're invincible
Yeah
Invisible to the truth
Of who you are
Or
Who love wants you to be
Hmmmmm

When you feel life inside
It gives you sheer lust
Of one's egotistical remains
Of the soul."

"Whooooo, go on girl!" Sarai yelled.
Cyfin continued.

"Feel that? Yeah.
Love
You know love comes knocking on your heart
Sometimes we answer the beat
But it's the door
To the wrong opportunity
But that's all right you see
Love can do that
Knock
It's always
The fabric of opportunity
Yeah love

Now as I listen to life
What is it saying?
Or yet
What will I say to it?

Listen to me
Love me, hold me
Never let me go
Until my soul can conquer no more
I end this quest of yearning for your love
You have to understand
We are all one, together
Realizing that love is knocking
Constantly . . . Knocking
Looooovvvvvvveeeeeee!"

The music slowly faded. Ecstatically, the crowd clapped.

Sarai nodded her head in awe and said, "That was awesome. When are you going to get up there?"

I looked at Cyfin as she walked off the stage and waved to a crowd of her friends.

"One day I plan to. One day."

By now, Nikki had brought me my second drink.

"Try this," Nikki said, handing me a drink.

"What is this?"

"It's a Ruby Hot Mama."

"A *what*?" Sarai and I asked together.

"A Ruby Hot Mama!"

We all laughed.

"It's on the house," Nikki said.

The drink was delicious, however, hearing the word "mama" made me think about my birth mother.

My mom left my dad and me when I was two. I really don't know much about her. My dad said she was strung out on drugs. My dad remarried another woman named Charity, but she died when I was 13. She was somewhat weird if you ask me. I don't know what my dad saw in her. Charity stayed in the bedroom with the door closed most of the time. She was extremely homely. I never introduced her to any of my friends. Many of them were shocked when they found out that I had a stepmother. One weekend my dad flew to Chicago to take care of business. He never told me what "business" he had there. Late Sunday night, on my way upstairs to my room, I heard the TV in my dad's bedroom. Charity never went to sleep with the TV on.

The bedroom door was slightly open.

"Charity!"

She didn't reply. Charity's pale skin looked ghostly as the static from the television screen casted its rays on her back. She had the same clothes on from yesterday, which was very unusual.

I yelled her name again.

"Charity!"

She didn't move. I shoved the bed with my knee. Now facing her, I realized she was dead. I took the small piece of paper from her hand and placed the note in my dad's drawer. My dad never mentioned Charity's name or her last whispers again.

"I really liked Cyfin," Sarai said.

"Yes. You said that already."

Sarai looked at me without continuing the conversation. I was afraid Doug told her what happened the second time I saw him after I moved in. I forgot where I was, and began to reminisce about the day I kissed Sarai's husband.

"It's good to see you again," Doug said, extending his hand.

I wanted to extend more than just a neighborly handshake. Inquisitively, he walked in my apartment.

"Did you move in here by yourself?"

I wanted to say yes with all my heart, but I didn't want to play games with a married man.

"No. My boyfriend and I moved in together."

"Oh, I see. Wait, you're not just saying that, are you?" Doug asked.

For the past couple of years I felt I was in a relationship by myself. Randy was preoccupied with everyone else. On his days off, he rarely spent time with me. I was a second priority. Sometimes I would stay out late with my friends and would still make it home before he did.

"Well, welcome anyway. You and your invisible 'boyfriend.' Maybe my wife and I could fix dinner for you and your boyfriend," Doug said.

"That would be great."

He continued to walk around my apartment. I watched his every move, contemplating on kissing his lips. I ignored the fact I had a stranger roaming around in my apartment. I followed his every move. The scent of his cologne made my hormones spiral like a blowing dandelion in the wind.

"We have the same layout as you, but we have a larger balcony!" Doug shouted from the hallway.

He walked back toward the living room and sat on the couch. He patted the sofa cushion next to him.

"Have a seat," he said.

"Have a seat? This is my apartment. I'm supposed to ask you to have a seat, which, by the way, I didn't."

He stood up and walked near the window facing the parking structure.

"Where did you say you were from?"

"I didn't."

I figured that if I acted as if I didn't care, he would leave and the temptation of lust would follow him out the door.

"Have I overstayed my welcome?"

I felt sorry.

"No. I feel really uncomfortable because you are married."

"Oh, I see. Does that mean I can't talk to you?"

"No, that's not what I meant."

I felt trapped inside of his box of passion. I walked past him on my way to open the door for him to leave. He met me halfway and smiled. My heart pounded 10 times faster. The attraction between us was apparent. He leaned over and gently kissed me. His lips were soft and warm. I forgot who I was and grabbed him back, tasting infidelity on his tongue.

"Well, I'll let you be," he said.

I didn't say a word. Mesmerized, I sat on the sofa, wondering what would happen if he hadn't left my apartment.

"Hello . . . Beauty! Come back to Earth!" Sarai exclaimed. "Girl, what were you thinking about? I was going on and on . . . and then I noticed you weren't paying me any attention!"

"Oh . . . nothing."

"I have a proposition for you—or my husband and I have a proposition for you," Sarai said.

I suddenly felt nervous while my body temperature rose.

Feeling sweat build under my arms, I said, "Sarai, what are you talking about?"

"Well, I've noticed Doug has admired you from day one. Last week he told me—"

"Told you what?"

"He told me about when he flirted with you when you first moved in. You know, we like to spice up our love life from time to time. And . . . well."

Sarai took a big gulp of her drink. I had a funny feeling where this conversation was going, only I wasn't prepared on how to end it.

"Would you be willing to engage us in the privacy of our lovemaking experience?" She asked candidly.

I didn't respond. I didn't know whether to laugh or change the subject. I saw a few movies about ménage á trios and none of them had a happy ending. The conversation made me very edgy.

DON'T CRY FOR LOVE

A few months ago, my womanly instincts were in an uproar. I knew Randy was up to no good. I came home and noticed Randy left his cell phone on the charger, which was rare. I pressed 'redial' on his cell phone. The call went to his voicemail without asking for the password. Flabbergasted by the easy access, his mailbox was full. Countless women left messages. I didn't recognize any of the few male voices. However, the last message I listened to was the worst one of all. I became infuriated.

A woman was upset with Randy because she didn't appreciate the fact that after their ménage á trios he tried to talk to her girlfriend. I couldn't believe my ears. She said he was lowdown and scandalous. She threatened he would get what he deserved.

Thinking about Sari's proposal, I replied, "Are you for real?"

"Yes. What do you say?" Sarai asked.

I hesitated, "I don't think so."

"This is not the first time we've done this, just to let you know," she said.

"Why are we talking about this?"

I choked on my drink. Thankfully that ended the conversation and I was relieved when a man came and asked if I was OK. I focused more on the stain on his shirt rather than his kind gesture. I told him everything was fine. My lack of interest in his conversation yielded his attention elsewhere.

Later that night, at home in my bed, I tossed and turned, thinking of the time I found a bag full of numbers and condoms in Randy's drawer. I was absolutely fed up, I thought.

He said, "Those are old! And why were you going through my stuff?"

My stomach turned inside out. I wanted Randy to leave, but he wanted to stay. I never met a man who lied so much, even God believed him.

It's funny how time lapses.
And you realize one day . . . Reality.
Sitting here listening to Luther Vandross,
I remember the day you proposed to me.
Why?
Why did you send me on a fantasy trip?
That you had no intentions on being a part of!
Listening to the song, I had picked to march down the eternal aisle of
love . . .
Why?
Why did you waste life's time, anticipating heartbreak?
And your non-committed self-love and self-hate
That I had no knowledge of.
Time will tell.
It will open up the doors to the truth.
The doors to the soul of reality.
I guess I am grateful to you.
Thank you for not marrying me.
Knowing how conniving, sneaky, and despicable you truly are!
A non-committed walking mammal!
Thanks for having my back!

CHAPTER SIX

I arrived at Teresa's apartment. Teresa and I met when my dad and I moved after Charity's death. I was a few years older than Teresa, but she always tried to boss me around as if she were the oldest. Teresa came over almost every night to have dinner with us. My dad dated her mom for a while. Their relationship ended when Teresa's dad moved back to Los Angeles. My dad considered Teresa to be one of his own. I didn't mind because Teresa kept me from being lonely.

There was a box near the front of the Teresa's apartment building. A piece of Kente cloth hung over the edge. I wanted to search the box, but changed my mind. I buzzed the button on the stucco wall and noticed the chipped wood trimmings. The sign "The Springs" needed more than a paint job. However, inside the building was beautiful.

"Who is it?" Teresa asked.

"Beauty!"

"You made it," she said.

The door opened. I looked back at the box again and noticed an envelope under the Kente cloth. For some reason I was drawn to it. I was about to walk toward the box, but stopped when I saw a kid coming my way on a skateboard. He passed the box and yelled "Hurry up!" to a young girl on a pink bike. The white basket on the front of the bike made me nostalgic. I thought about the first bike my dad bought me. Out of all the bikes I ever had, it was my favorite one. The basket on my bike was white, but it had a pink flower in the middle. I kept my Barbie and money for the doughnut man in there. I couldn't wait to hear the horn from the doughnut truck. He drove cautiously down the street in his dull green van and had every doughnut imaginable. My dad counted on me to get his favorite. He liked plain glaze and I liked the long chocolate bars. Charity didn't care for them at all. After the kids passed by, I lifted the Kente cloth. There was almost $300 in a blank envelope. There were also a few CDs, boxers, and T-shirts, too. I walked back to the door and rang the buzzer again.

"Beauty, is that you?" Teresa asked.

"Yes."

"Wesley and I were about to come look for you," Teresa said laughing.

Wesley was Teresa's .22 pistol. I walked in the building. In front, there was an elevator immediately to the left and another one near the back. The porcelain tile that shined on the floor and the waterfall made the lobby breathtaking. Kids were often heard before seen in the pool near the front, as this pool had a diving board and Jacuzzi. Near every elevator were beautiful miniature palm trees.

When I got off the elevator, I saw Teresa standing outside her door.

"You missed it. I just kicked Satan out!" She exclaimed.

Satan was our nickname for Teresa's boyfriend. His real name was Eldon. He committed many crimes that I told Teresa he was Satan's apprentice. Therefore, we always referred to Eldon as Satan.

"He told me he 'accidentally' got Shelia pregnant," Teresa continued.

"Accidentally? Doesn't she live next door to him?"

"Yes! Can you believe it? If I ever run into her . . . "

Teresa was livid.

"I don't care if I'm old, decrepit, and on a cane, she's mine!" She continued to say.

"Calm down."

"I put the little stuff he had here in a big box outside. Did you see it?"

I paused for a minute.

"Yes. I found nearly $300 in an envelope!"

"I know. I put it in there. You can have it. I don't want anything of his in this apartment. If it weren't you, someone else would've taken it. Anyway Beauty, I need a manicure. Do you want to ride with me over to Fancy Nails? I hope Linda is available," she said.

"Sure. I need a pedicure. My big toe needs some attention," I said extending my foot.

We both frowned at the receding toe nail polish. I made my way to the sofa and noticed a picture of Randy, Teresa, and myself. Tears trickled down my face. Teresa came and held me in her arms. I cried like I'd never cried before.

"I don't know why you didn't let me come with you to Randy's funeral," Teresa said.

I didn't feel like responding, I had no intentions on reliving Randy's funeral service. I decided to take a short nap while Teresa took a shower.

"Ouch!" I groaned.

Teresa ran from the bathroom.

"Are you OK? What's wrong?"

I looked at Teresa with my mouth slightly open and shrugged my shoulders and said, "I guess I was dreaming."

On the way to the car, we saw Farah. Farah used to hang out with us all the time, until she met Stack. She met him while he was in Navy training. Farah wrote Stack every week. Farah wasn't America's Next Top Model, but she definitely could keep herself looking better. She was proud Stack was her boyfriend, and he could do no wrong. Stack came to visit Farah whenever he had the opportunity, and after a few visits, Farah was pregnant. Somehow, Stack neglected to tell Farah he already had four kids. I warned Farah that Stack seemed sneaky. With all my experience with Randy's shenanigans, she didn't believe me.

Two years later, when Farah was pregnant with Stack's second child, so was Rebecca. Rebecca, from what Teresa said, lived around the corner from Stacks' mother's house in Oakland. Farah and Rebecca had their sons around the same month. Rumor had it that Rebecca was pregnant again.

"Farah, did you kick Stack out and get your key?" I asked.

I knew the answer was no, but I had to ask. Her facial expression confirmed my assumption.

"Please. At least I know where Stack is, upstairs at home. How about your boyfriend? Where's Randy, or should I say who is he with right now? Oh, I forgot . . . he's dead," Farah replied.

"I can't believe you said that," Teresa intervened.

Farah hurt my feelings for good. I held back my words and never spoke to her again.

These tears I shed
Are dedicated to you
You've given me strength and courage
To make it through

You standing by my side
I will never ever forget
God has truly blessed you
With full of wit

I need you by my side
Please stand strong

DON'T CRY FOR LOVE

Please forgive me now
If I've ever said anything wrong

You and I together
Is what we need
Together let's grow
God-fearing and planting seeds

Remember this
My beloved sweetheart
I've always had your back
From the very start

Unified through God
Our bond will be
I'll forever pray
For you and me

CHAPTER SEVEN

There were no seats left at Joi's again. I decided to enjoy this night by myself. It's been two months since Randy's death and I continued to think of him every day. He was the core in my earth's crust.

I stopped reminiscing of Randy when I saw Nikki stop and talk to the "man at the booth." I tried to suppress my nervousness, but I couldn't take my eyes away from their conversation. Every time I saw the "man at the booth," butterflies would flutter in my stomach because he was very stylish and handsome. I was drawn to him like bees to honey. To distract my thoughts, I contemplated on reciting a poem. I wanted to introduce the world to my stage name, Floetic Mystress.

Meanwhile, a new poet took the stage.

"Hey everybody, my name is Sizzle. The name of my poem is '*Can't Take It,*'" she said.

Sizzle captured my attention. Her long bone-straight hair with a part down the middle reminded me of Disney's Pocahontas.

"Damn I'm tired
Of my boyfriend's sh*t
Messing around with these females
Hittin' licks.

SHAR STURGES

He thinks I don't know the real.
Sometimes I feel like
Just takin' a hit
Right in his pretty little grill.

One day he's gonna look up
And I'll be gonna
Not looking back
While he's kickin' stones.

I've been through it all
You won't believe
Getting a woman pregnant
A thought I still can't conceive.

I wish he would be real
Marry me and settle down
But nope, he wants to set trip
And act like a freaking clown.

But I guess
I'll never see that day
I'll keep hope
Trying to play all the way

Still finding numbers
Bringing women to the pad
Can't take this no more
Tired of feelin' sad.

Can't hang in there
Not for one more day
He never listens
To what I have to say.

I give up
Completely, I'm done
I love you dearly,
But you ain't the one.

I'm walkin' away
Alone once again
Keepin' my hustle on
Being real to the end."

Every woman in the house, including me, gave a standing ovation. She made me feel as if I should have left Randy a long time ago. I was tired of running from my problems. Feeling empowered, I forgot about the handsome "man at the booth." I wanted all men to feel every woman's pain. Desensitized to my true feelings, thoughts ricocheted from Sizzle to me.

Tonight reminded me of many nights I'd stay up waiting for Randy to come home. Maybe I'll never be able to accept his death. The thunder roared like a hungry lion. I pulled the covers over my head and closed my eyes. My childhood fear crept as the rain pelted on the window. Instantly, it felt as if someone was sitting on Randy's side of the bed. My heart raced with fear. I heard a voice whisper.

"Beauty, I will never leave your side."

Frightened, I closed my eyes. Something pulled the covers from my body with force. I jumped from my bed, slipped, and fell. I hit my head on the rail. The alarm sounded. I awoke and noticed I was still in the bed with the covers neatly tucked in place.

Relieved from my dream, I reached for the remote, turned on the TV, and tuned into a comedy show.

"Howard, what are you doing here?" The woman on the sitcom said.

Howard! I forgot all about him. Howard Tendell, life before Randy. The moment I saw Howard, the moment our eyes met, our attraction burned instantly like the flame on a match. Breathless, his eyes undressed my soul and stripped me away.

"I know you may hear this a lot, but you are beautiful. I mean, I'm not trying to pick up on you at a gas station. OK wait. Honestly, yes I am. I can't describe what I'm feeling," Howard said.

I was speechless.

"I don't normally pick up on women at the gas station, but I'm drawn to you. Please tell me your name, my beautiful flower."

I swallowed the smell of passion and replied, "Beauty."

"How ironic, that name suits you well. My name is Howard," he said as he extended his hand.

I noticed his clean fingernails and huge hands. He grabbed my hand and gently kissed it. The annoying honking caused us both to turn as a man gestured for Howard to move his car.

"Hey buddy, are you going to get gas or what?" The man yelled.

Howard motioned for the impatient man to wait.

"Beauty, I really would like to see you again. Do you think that would be possible?"

"Yeah. Sure."

"Wait here. I'm going to see if I can find a piece of paper and a pen. The battery's dead in my cell phone."

I unhooked the gas pump from my car and placed it back on the latch. Howard walked over to the man in the car. The stranger looked at me and smiled. I wondered if they both saw the word "desperate" dangle over my head. Howard walked over to the gas station attendant seated behind a glass window. He turned toward me and walked with a piece of paper and pen in hand. That's when I noticed Howard had beady eyes. My dad always told me, "Never trust anyone with beady eyes." I chuckled.

"Beauty, here is my number," Howard said, writing his number on half of the paper. He tore the paper a little bit below his number and gave me both sheets. I wrote my number on the blank sheet, folded the torn sheet in half, and placed it in his hand. I rolled his fingers halfway toward his palm, as if giving my number to him was a secret. I walked toward the driver side of my car and opened the door. The moment felt magical I didn't want it to end.

"It was nice meeting you, Mr. Howard."

I didn't give him a chance to respond. I flopped in the car and left. That night Howard called. He said he didn't want to seem as if he was stalking me, but he could not wait to talk to me. I confessed to Howard I felt the same way. We made plans to hang out at the amusement park the next day. Before I knew it, I was over Howard's loft. Weekend after weekend, we made love in every room. We even drove to Las Vegas on a four-day weekend trip. We talked practically every day. Howard was too good to be true.

"Beauty, I could see us growing old together," Howard said.

"Really? Wow, I never thought about marriage, let alone growing old with someone."

"Who said anything about marriage?"

"Well, I . . . "

Howard grabbed me forcibly and kissed my lost thoughts away.

"Beauty, you know I'm just playing, right?"

If the future could've warned me, I wished I would've asked which part was a joke: marriage or the entire relationship.

Before I knew it, Howard and I dated for a few months. For some strange reason, I realized I didn't know Howard's last name. I called Howard during my break as I usually did and his cell phone went straight to voicemail. I finally had enough courage to tell him I was expecting his child. Although, I wasn't sure if I would keep the baby. I desperately needed to talk to him. I called his house phone. There was no answer. I called his cell phone again and left a message. Two days after Howard's disappearance I decided to call the police. There was one problem: I didn't know Howard's last name. I decided to call his cell phone one last time. This time a woman answered. I quickly hung up. I guess Howard was too good to be true because he belonged to someone else.

My cell phone rang. It was Howard. Hesitantly I answered.

"Hello."

"You just called this number?" The inquisitive woman asked.

"Your voice is not the one I wanted to hear."

"This is Detective Stern. Are you calling for Mr. Howard Tendell?"

"Detective Stern?"

Whatever happened, I didn't want to get involved. All my life, my dad protected me from any involvement with the police, despite the many times they raided our house.

"Ma'am, please don't hang up. We need your help," the detective said.

I laughed and thought how the police wanted my help. Clearly, this detective was unaware I was the daughter of "Badluck" Chuck.

"Ma'am, Mr. Tendell is wanted for rape and murder in several different counties. We have reason to believe he was staging you as his next victim."

I couldn't believe my ears. My fingers and legs became numb. I dropped the phone and ran to the toilet. A few days later, I had an abortion and changed my number. I never told Randy about Howard or the pregnancy. I didn't utter his name again. I practically erased him from my memory, until now.

I turned the television off. Once again, I felt pain in my stomach. I needed medicine. Thanks to my dad, I always had a supply of Vicodin. I turned over and lay on my side. I noticed a few dried roses on the dresser I'd kept from my last birthday. Randy woke me up the morning of my birthday. Balloons floated on the ceiling, and there was a banner that read "Happy Birthday."

Pink and red rose petals lay haphazardly in a trail from the bedroom to the kitchen. I followed the silk roses and found a cake propped on the kitchen table. Written on the cake was "Happy Birthday, with Much Love." A wrapped present was adjacent to the cake box. I grabbed the gift and tore through the paper. I opened the blue velvet jewelry box. The diamond stud earrings sparkled like stars twinkling in the sky.

Randy serenaded me, "Happy Birthday Beauty."

He couldn't hold a note to save his life, which made the moment quite comical. His gestures and facial fluctuations were hilarious. He cooked me a delicious breakfast, scrambled eggs with potatoes, bell peppers, diced chicken, mushrooms, and melted cheese. It was Randy's famous breakfast recipe. He served breakfast to me in bed. After he put the breakfast tray on the bed, he handed me a vase full of long-stem roses. He had a mug made with our picture embroidered with hearts. Randy was a hopeless romantic to me—and to every other woman as well, I later realized.

CHAPTER EIGHT

I'm tired of these dreadful tears
Of love's lies and games
When will it all fit together?
Like the pieces of a puzzle
Twenty-five years into life
And I don't want to grow old
All by my lonesome
This can't be for me
Lonely, I lay across my bed
I can't continue
To walk down
This empty road of loneliness
Having a man and being lonely
I must be crazy!
The man I want . . . cheats
The man I should've married . . . is married
And the one I dream of doesn't know I'm alive . . .

felt as if I was stuck in misery, and I missed misery's company. I'm glad Teresa called and asked me to come over. She said she wanted me to go with her to run an errand. That meant my dad and her were in cahoots.

My dad and Teresa worked together. For whatever reason, they both sought to keep me out of their business affairs, which I didn't mind. They talked in code. I never repeated what I heard in fear I might say the wrong thing. One night I heard my dad tell Donald, his best friend, "The sheep will jump over the fence tonight." When the opportunity arose, I asked my dad what that meant. He told me never to repeat what I heard and never explained what that statement meant.

On my way to the car, I started to think about the "man at the booth." The next time I went to Joi's, I hoped he would be there. I wanted to know his name. I wanted to hear his voice. I felt my veins tie into knots, thinking about the "man at the booth." The anticipation was unbearable. I had to get to Joi's tonight.

Suddenly, I remembered I felt the same way the day I met Randy. I was ecstatic when I first saw him. It felt as though we had known each other for years.

My thoughts of Randy were interrupted when the elevator door opened.

"Hi Beauty," Sarai said as she stepped into the elevator.

"Hey Sarai."

"Tonight my husband won't be home and I'm in need of some R&R. Are you going to Joi's tonight?"

"Yes. I was just thinking about going. Be ready by nine."

"OK Beauty, I'll see you then." She managed to speak while the elevator doors closed.

When I arrived at Teresa's I rang her buzzer. It took a few minutes before she responded.

"Hi Teresa, it's me."

I heard a man's voice in the background. His voice sounded like Stack, Farrah's boyfriend. Teresa spoke through the intercom.

"I'll buzz you in."

I tried to inquire about the man's voice, but she didn't reply. When I arrived at her door, it was ajar. Teresa was in her bathrobe. The shower water deflected my attention, as there was no steam coming from the bathroom.

"Who was that I heard in the background?"

"You didn't hear anyone, unless it was the TV," Teresa said as she pointed to the male news anchor.

"The TV. Yeah, OK."

"I was just about to take a shower. Make yourself at home. You know this is your second home. Mi casa es su casa," she said as she pranced away.

I smacked my lips, slid onto the leather chaise, and drifted to sleep. The sharp pains in my stomach became worse. I heard muffled voices, but I couldn't see anyone. Someone grabbed my hand. I tried to open my eyes, but for some reason I couldn't. My fingers twitched. I desperately tried to lift my hand, but remained motionless.

"Wake up, Beauty! Let's go. Beauty! Wake up!"

A voice became familiar.

"Teresa, is that you?"

"Well who do you think it is? God?"

I stared at Teresa, contemplating if it were a dream.

"Beauty, I think you really need a vacation," Teresa said.

We arrived at a park. I saw a few children playing tag. I thought about the times my dad dropped me off at his best friend, Donald's house. Donald and his wife Susan had two children, Althea and Bailey. Althea was extremely boy crazy. In fact, she taught me everything there was to know about sex, I thought. My first crush was on her older brother Bailey. He told me I was like his little sister. I hated when he said that. I thought he was the cutest boy who walked the face of the earth. Every time I saw him, I dreamed of our first kiss. Fireworks burst in the sky whenever I saw him. The crackling sound of my heartbeat sent chills through my body.

One day, I decided to tell Bailey how I felt.

"Beauty, when you grow up you will be beautiful, just like your name," Bailey said.

I melted. If only I were old enough to be his girlfriend. He gently leaned over and kissed me on my forehead.

"You are just too young," he continued to say.

That's when I realized I had fallen in love with a gentleman.

Teresa shoved my arm.

"That's her!" Teresa yelled.

"That's who?"

"You're asking too many questions."

What was this? Mission Impossible? I looked next to the children running in circles around a tree. I saw a young girl siting on a bench, suspiciously looking around. Her bright T-shirt stood out like a raven among doves.

"Walk over there and ask her, 'did the duck die?' "

I laughed.

"What?" I asked.

"Beauty, listen. I'm going to drive around the block with her. Be ready when I get back. Don't go anywhere. Stay put. You know how you like to wander," Teresa said.

"That's it? That's all I'm good for?"

I had no intentions of wanting to do more. I was as nervous as a kid was on her first day of school. I turned back to Teresa for assurance. She reached toward the glove compartment. I promised myself I would never put myself in this position again. Whatever my dad and Teresa did no longer concerned me. The girl looked at me as if she heard my every thought. I walked closer in her direction. She didn't look as young as I thought. She was in her late thirties. Paranoid, the young woman grabbed her bag and stood up. I approached the young woman and asked her what Teresa instructed me to do.

"Did the duck die?"

I wanted to laugh, but I knew this was no laughing matter. I managed to conceal my emotions. Without saying a word, the woman walked over to Teresa's car and opened the door. Fear on her face confirmed my leeriness as Teresa drove away. That's when I noticed the front and back plates were missing from Teresa's car. She had a bogus car dealer advertisement in the place of the license plates.

I didn't know what to do. I froze in my tracks. I watched the birds circle above flying like vultures waiting for their next victim. I walked over to the bench and sat on the opposite side of another woman. My back faced the children playing. I didn't want anyone to sense my fear. I put my head in my hands and closed my eyes. I couldn't take the agony any longer. When I looked across the street, there was a taxicab at the gas station. I didn't ponder my situation for another moment. I jaywalked across the street.

"Are you in service?"

He nodded and gestured for me to get in the cab. Relieved, I gave him my address.

I didn't call Teresa when I arrived home. She tried to call me on my cell phone, but I wasn't prepared to hear what she had to say. I slouched in my couch and reflected on the day's journey. There was a knock at the door. I was not in the mood for any company. I looked through the peephole. It was Sarai. I opened the door.

"Girl, you know you are not supposed to open the door without asking who it is. I could've been a masked murder! And why are you sitting here in the dark, Beauty?"

She didn't give me a chance to respond before she continued.

"Do you miss Randy? Why aren't you getting ready to go to Joi's? Did you forget? Are we still going?"

"Yes Sarai. Yes to all your questions. I'll be over in a few minutes."

Sarai gave me a hug. Tears fell. I ached. My soul felt empty. The room temperature dropped. The picture Randy and I took fell to the floor. Sarai and I screamed and remained glued to each other. We never spoke about what we experienced the night I cried my hurt away. I needed to start a new life, one with new opportunities, and no regrets. Randy was in the past. I was ready for the future. For just one night, I wanted my life to be drama free.

Like a bird whose lost its feather
We've become distant to the weather
I'm a shooting star
You've left by far

How can we mend what we had?
For you, I think our love was just a fad
I've waited and I've waited for you
But once again, our love isn't true

Softly and deeply my love continues to grow
Somehow, you seem to never know

DON'T CRY FOR LOVE

As the years pass by
I'm flying high
High away from your lies

Forget me not, forget me
I was yours for eternity
Never again once more
I continue to pour

My head is full of your lies
I'm wiping away my tear-filled eyes
Goodbye dear sweet pain . . .
I'm letting go of this cloud of rain

CHAPTER NINE

When Sarai and I arrived at Joi's, I saw the "man at the booth" standing at the door as we entered. He was a several feet taller than me.

"Is that him? The 'man at the booth?' " Sarai asked.

"I tell you way too much of my personal business."

"Yeah, Beauty. Sure you do. Are you going to at least say hi to the guy?"

"Why?"

"Beauty, are you for real! This guy is gorgeous, and from where I'm standing, he seems available. There is no woman holding on to his arm. There is no wedding ring or ring tan on his ring finger, unless he's gay."

"Sarai!"

We both laughed. I was nervous as we walked his way. He looked right in my direction. Butterflies danced in my stomach.

"Hello," he said.

His voice soothed my soul. His light brown eyes, thick eyebrows, and a deep dimple in his left cheek sent a sexy sensation of lust through me. Too timid to speak, I smiled. Preparing to sit in my chair, Sarai hit me on my arm.

"Beauty, you couldn't at least say hi?"

I turned and looked to my left. Then I turned and looked to my right.

"Oh, for a moment I thought my mama was here!"

"Beauty. Come on! At least see what the man has to offer."

I agreed with Sarai's every word.

"You're right. I mean, I'll never get over Randy, but I can't live my life holding my breath in sorrow and pity."

My own advice sounded good, but I felt as if I could never trust another or love no other like Randy Henderson.

"That's it, Beauty. That's the spirit. I'll go ask him to join us," Sarai said, pushing back her chair.

"No!" I whispered and grabbed her wrist.

"If it's meant for us to talk, I'm quite sure he will make it happen."

"Beauty, I don't know what world you're living in, but I'm going to live in it with you tonight."

As soon as Sarai made her statement, the lights dimmed. A song by Aretha Franklin, "*I Never Loved a Man (The Way I Love You)*" played. The words to her song were exactly what I felt. I downloaded the song to my phone as the lights slightly appeared brighter. A skinny young man with a short haircut appeared on stage. He wore a polo shirt with an argyle sweater tied around his neck.

"Hey y'all, listen up, my name is Titus, and I have a story to tell."

Animated, he swayed his head and arms as he talked.

"See let me tell you
Why he's so fly
I was standing in the club
When he walked his pretty little self by

Twitching and swinging
His hands and body
I just knew
He was gonna be a part of me

DON'T CRY FOR LOVE

Don't get it twisted
Just 'cause I'm gay
Oh well, la de da
Like Burger King, I'll have it my way

Voguing and dancing
Is what he did best
But I was oh so destined
To put his love skills to the test

I pranced on over
To the sweet boy's direction
I couldn't prevent
From getting an erection

But needless to say
I tapped him on the side
He turned and looked at me
Then I punched him in the eye

I'd realized that was Joe
Whom I was with for a year
But he was mad
'Cause I filled him with fear

Three months ago
He got my sister pregnant
I keeps it real
That's why he got knocked in his pretty little grill

Flamboyant I may be
But so what
Don't hate
'Cause I have a soft strut

And don't judge me
Or even try to be rude
'Cause I gots' drama
Just like you!"

As the lights crawled to a faint vision, the candles beautifully burned on the tables. Titus dropped the microphone as the rest of Aretha's song played. Titus received a standing ovation. I clapped, and noticed the "man at the booth" staring at me. I smiled and waved.

Aretha's song faded and the lights were bright. Joi walked on stage.

"I know one thing, you guys are going to quit dropping my microphone," Joi said as she laughed and placed the microphone back on the stand.

"We will have Cyfin come on stage in a bit with '*Cool Brutha Stroll*,'" Joi said.

I spoke to Cyfin the last time she was here and told her how I was a huge fan. She was very charismatic. She asked me the infamous question everyone did:

"Beauty, when are you going to get on stage?"

I explained to her about my stage fright. She went on to say she had the very same fear. In fact, she said she still gets nervous from time to time. She said her secret was to have a couple of drinks before she performed. I didn't want to start that habit. After our conversation, I felt a little better.

"Beauty, here comes the 'man from the booth,' " Sarai said.

"Sarai, quit playing."

"No Beauty. Really. Turn around. He's headed over here!"

Sarai joked around all the time. I didn't embrace her enthusiasm. The "man at the booth" walked right past us and went to the bar.

"See Sarai, you would have had me in a huff! I knew he wasn't coming this way."

"Well, he did. He just decided to keep walking," she said as we laughed.

A few minutes later, Nikki came over with a couple of drinks.

"Hey Beauty and Sarai, here are complimentary drinks from the gentleman at the bar."

It was the "man at the booth!"

"Are you for real Nikki? Nikki, for real?" I inquired.

"Yes Beauty. He said if you accept his drink, that would be his cue to come over and introduce himself. He also said if you're not interested, he would understand, but you could still have the drink."

"If I take the drink, and I'm not interested, how will he know?"

"Oh, he told me to give him a thumb's-down signal."

We all laughed. I took the drink and Nikki walked away.

"That girl has a good memory. She remembered my name! Oh, she's getting a real good tip. Now I can say this with sureness, the "man at the booth" is on his way over here," Sarai said quickly.

Indeed he was. He walked toward our table.

"Smile, Beauty!" Sarai quickly whispered.

"Hello beautiful ladies. How are you?" He asked.

"I'm fine," I answered.

Sarai didn't say a word. She was too busy kicking my toe.

"Allow me to introduce myself. My name is Breeze. Well, my real name is Owen, but everyone calls me Breeze."

"Hello Mr. Owen. Please join us," Sarai said.

I kicked her foot back.

"Thank you. I hope I'm not interrupting," he said as he looked directly into my eyes.

I was in heaven. I did not want to return to Earth, unless Breeze was with me. I couldn't bring myself to say very much. The moment was like a dream. It was too good to be true.

"I'm Sarai and this is Beauty." I kicked Sarai's foot again. This time she kicked back and bumped the table.

"Whoa," Breeze said.

"Oh, sorry, I caught a cramp in my foot," Sarai said.

"You know Beauty, I see you in here all the time. You've been coming here for a while."

"Yeah, I love coming to Joi's. I've seen you in here, too."

Cyfin took the stage.

"All right, tonight we have an interactive poem. For those of you who went to public school like me that means this will require your participation," Cyfin said.

The crowd whispered awes and snarls.

"I'm just kidding. Relax. OK. When I say 'cool brutha stroll', I want you to say it with me. Let's give it a try."

The crowd in unison said, "cool brutha stroll."

"Come on, I can't hear you!" Cyfin yelled with her right hand cupped over her ear.

"Cool brutha stroll," everyone said.

"Cool brutha stroll," Cyfin said as she gestured to the crowd to say it with her.

"Your walk,
My soul
Makes we wonder
How I got over

DON'T CRY FOR LOVE

Your talk
Your swag
Your strut
Your do-rag
My wedding ring . . . Oh

You walk the walk
You talk the talk
Makes we wanna holla,
And begin to stalk you
All day long
Singin' my song
'Cause of your
Cool brutha stroll

You can't emulate it
You can't hater-aid it
You can't substitute it
'Cause my brutha
Homie, lover, friend
Always walkin'
Against the wind, swoosh.

Cool brutha stroll
Don't wanna take control
I wanna hold your hand,
Through it all
Standin' 10 feet tall
Knockin' down walls
With your cool brutha stroll

I stare, I sit
I walk with a twitch
To get a glimpse of you
Don't stop
Don't flop
No wiggle in your walk
'Cause that's a cool brutha's stroll."

The crowd went ballistic, from sneers to cheers.

"What's up with all this twitchin' talk?" Sarai said.

"What are you talking about?" I asked.

"Both poets Cyfin and Titus talked about twitching. I don't twitch. I glide," Sarai said prancing in her seat, raising both her arms, and swaying from side to side.

"Whoa, I definitely wasn't paying any attention to that!" Breeze said.

"Please, don't entertain her Breeze. I'm driving us home Sarai."

Breeze and I laughed even harder.

"I think it's time for us to leave."

"Here, let me help you," Breeze said.

Breeze stood up and pulled my seat out. We both paused for a moment. Breathing the same air, we smiled. He gestured for hug. I gave in. Sarai interrupted us by clearing her throat.

"My bad," Breeze said as he walked toward Sarai to help her out of her seat.

I shook my head and smiled. Sarai could barely stand up. I forgot she had a few drinks before Breeze sent drinks to our table. Breeze walked back to me.

"Beauty, is it OK if I get your number?" he asked.

"Sure. I can call you on your cell."

"I left my phone at home, but if you tell me your number, I will remember. I hope we can enjoy each other's company outside of the ambiance of Joi's," Breeze said.

"Breeze, if you remember my number, the pleasure will be all mine."

Sarai chimed in, "Beauty that was spoken like a true poet."

The night ended just how I ventured - for a new opportunity and to be drama-free.

CHAPTER TEN

It felt like days had gone by since I last saw Breeze. I hadn't been to Joi's for a week. These cramps I've experienced have made me lazy as hell. My cell phone vibrated. I looked at the caller ID. The number was blocked.

"Hello!"

There was no sound. Right before I pushed the end button, "Beauty! It's good to hear your voice."

"Breeze?"

"The one and only!"

My heart marched to Breeze's rhythm of love.

Trying not to sound infatuated, "You remembered my number?"

I didn't know if I was asking a question or making a statement.

"Of course I did. Honestly, it took me a few days because I wanted to clear my calendar just for you for the weekend. Would you like to go out on a date with me? I . . . "

"Sure," quickly speaking without letting Breeze finish his sentence.

"You didn't let me tell you when and where," he chuckled.

"Surprise me. Just tell me what I should wear."

"Well, that's kind of hard to do, Beauty. Don't you know how to dress yourself?

"Breeze. I mean, should I dress casual, formal, or what?"

"Well. Since you want to be surprised, just plan for this - be ready by 10:30 a.m. Sunday morning. Wear something semi-dressy."

"OK. Sounds great. Breeze?"

"Yeah?"

"Why does it sound like you're running?"

"Because I am. Every Saturday morning I work out on the Santa Monica stairs."

"Oh."

"I'll let you get back to your beauty rest, Beauty."

"Ha ha ha. I'm wide-awake. I can tell you this, Mr. Breeze. I look forward to our date tomorrow."

"Me too. Bye my beautiful Beauty."

"Bye Breeze."

Smiling I ended the call. *I have a date with Breeze, on Sunday, at 10:30 a.m. I can hardly wait.*

"Beauty! I've been calling you! Why haven't you answered your cell phone? Were you ignoring my calls? Why are you tripping? Why did you leave the park? I told you to stay put!" Teresa yelled.

I don't know why Sarai and Teresa thought they were my mothers. Between the two of them, I think they scolded me more than my dad.

"Teresa, please. What's up?"

"What's up? OK Beauty, don't ask to come with me to make a drop anymore. I knew you weren't going to be there when I came back. I just knew it. What if I needed you, Beauty? You just don't bail out like that. Not like that Beauty. Not like that."

Teresa was right. I remembered when I was mad at Randy and I asked her to slash his tires the day after I heard the message about Randy's ménage à trois.

"Beauty! Beauty!" Randy yelled as he slammed the front door closed.

Startled I said, "What, Randy? I'm right here."

"What's wrong with you?" he asked. "I'm the one who's upset because somebody slashed my tires while I was at work. I had to call AAA to tow me to the auto shop down the street, so I could get two new tires!"

"What do you mean Randy, your tires were slashed?"

"I went outside to go to my car and I noticed my two back tires were slashed."

"What? Are you serious? What girl did you piss off?" I asked, trying not to sound guilty.

"What are you talking about? See, there you go, always turning situations around. I think I know who did it."

"Who?"

I was curious to hear his explanation.

"I know exactly who did it. It was those guys I got into it with last week in the parking lot."

Randy was rambling on and on. I tuned him out, wondering how I wish I could tell him I had his tires slashed because I was tired of him telling me he wasn't cheating, when I had concrete evidence that he was not faithful.

"Well, I'm glad you're OK," I said, smirking as I reached for the remote.

I think I had become a better liar than Randy. Thanks to Teresa, she had my back once again. Revenge felt sweet.

"Teresa, you're right. You know I have your back. The whole situation seemed uncomfortable. I'm sorry."

"It's all good in the hood."

"It's all what? Where did you pick that up? That sounds like something Stack would say."

"Stack? What would make you say such a thing, Beauty?"

"OK Teresa. What have you done? I know you like a book. What aren't you telling me?"

"Ha!"

She blurted and paused. Her silence of guilt was her sole confession.

"Beauty. You're crazy and I'm not about to entertain your fantasy."

"Oh yeah! You're busted. You sound guilty."

"Anyway Beauty," Teresa said, evading the accusations. "Are you busy today?"

"Nope."

"Come over and let's have a girls' day. We'll watch movies and hang out at Joi's."

"That sounds fun. Maybe that will take my mind off Breeze. I'll be there around noon. I'll tell you all about our date we have planned for tomorrow."

"He called you and you didn't call to tell me!"

"Teresa. He just called right before you did."

"Oh. Well get over here and we'll order some pizza. I'll see you when you get here, Beauty."

"OK. Bye."

When I arrived at Teresa's, she asked me what movie I wanted to watch. I really wasn't sure. I couldn't take my mind off Breeze and his infectious smile. I lost my focus. Teresa recommended a movie called *Anna Lucasta*. She said it was a black and white movie with Sammy Davis Jr. and Eartha Kitt. She teased me because I asked her who Eartha Kitt was. She made me remember that she was the older woman in *Boomerang* who tried to seduce Marcus. I didn't have the heart to tell her I was not into black and white movies.

As the movie played, I tried not to seem too anxious to talk about Breeze, but Teresa did not let the moment pass. I told her how he approached the table where Sarai and I sat. Teresa laughed uncontrollably when I told her about Sarai and I kicking each other under the table.

"Breeze probably thought you guys were weird."

"Who knows?"

"Did you sleep with him?"

"What! Where did that come from! I barely know the guy!" I exclaimed, throwing the pillow I leaned on at Teresa.

I don't know why Teresa made that remark. However, that discussion opened up some skeletons in both our closets. I told Teresa how I slept with Sarai's husband, Doug. She said that she could not believe I would do such a thing. I couldn't believe I did, either. I told her it happened the week Randy went with his friends on a skiing trip to Big Sur. Teresa confessed to me that the real reason her ex-boyfriend broke up with her was because she got pregnant, and she told him it wasn't his. She said since she didn't know who the father was she decided to term the pregnancy. After we cried and wiped our history away, we started watching the movie again. As Anna Lucasta smoked a cigarette while leaning on the bar, I remembered when Randy and I went to see our first movie together.

I told Randy I wanted to take him out on a date. He really didn't believe in letting me have control. He offered to come and pick me up. I wanted to pick him up and show him a great time. I knew he liked action movies. I surprised him and took him to Sebastian's. Sebastian's was a theater that showed movies before the release date to the public. The tickets were costly, but well worth it. I loved the chicken fingers with Sebastian's dipping sauce.

There were four viewing rooms. Each room had a theme. Hollywood Favorites was the name of one of them. This room was very posh with leather seating. Each chair reclined and had a personal beverage tray for each moviegoer. The next viewing room was Home Again. This room had a cozy living room setting. A faux fireplace greeted you when you walked in. I didn't get a chance to see the other two viewing rooms.

Our movie played in the Hollywood Favorites. We snuck into Home Again to watch another movie and shared our first kiss. Randy could not believe I had tickets to Sebastian's. I never told him they were an old gift from Howard.

Teresa interrupted my thinking, "Beauty, I can't believe we just watched two movies!"

"Don't you mean two movies just watched us?"

"What time are we going to Joi's?" Teresa asked.

Before I could answer, my cell phone rang. I pulled it out of my front pocket. There was a blocked number. Again, I was hesitant to answer, but I had a feeling it was Breeze.

"Hello."

"Hey Beauty."

"Breeze, you know when you call your number is blocked. Usually, I don't answer unidentified calls."

"Yeah, I forgot about that. That's why I'm calling. I think in haste of our conversation, I never gave you my number."

"Why don't you just unblock it?"

"If only it were that simple. I'll tell you all about it tomorrow. Tonight I won't be at Joi's, but I wanted you to know I'll be thinking of you."

I signaled for Teresa to leave the room. Glued to her seat, she ignored my request. I typed both Breeze's cell and home phone number into my contacts on my phone. When we hung up, Teresa said she didn't like the fact that he had a blocked number. I didn't have any major reservations about Breeze. For one reason or another, I trusted him.

CHAPTER ELEVEN

Teresa and I got dressed and drove to Joi's. She was unusually quiet. I asked her what was wrong, but she never confessed. We pulled into the parking lot. I looked for Breeze and remembered that he said he wasn't going to be there. Saddened, I realized I wanted to go home. Ever since Breeze introduced himself, the ambiance at Joi's changed. For some strange reason, I needed him at Joi's.

Nikki came over as soon as we sat at my favorite table. Teresa didn't order anything to drink, which baffled me. Teresa always had a drink or two. Since she didn't order anything, I didn't either and I didn't question it.

A few poets performed. The first was Thunder, who recited her poem. She was a tall, slender woman. She grabbed the microphone and looked at the ceiling. From a glance, she looked like supermodel Naomi Campbell. I closed my eyes and swayed side to side in rhythm of the background music.

"I place my hands between my thighs
I take a smell of what's inside.
Lying beside my faithful self
Indulging in life's walls of wealth

Taste the sweet of love and pain
Removing all the hurts and the stains

Kiss me high, kiss me low
Never seem to let me go

Wishing love would stop
But I'm high, I forget to ask why
Take me away to a pool of lust
Come get some of my sweet stuff
Of pleasure
Beads of sweat begin to pour
Onto the open wide floor
Sharing my thoughts of you
As my inside begins to brew

The love of you, the love of me
Climbs the stairs of ecstasy
One, two, three
Holding the pillow to muffle the screams

Can't explain it
One way or another
I've gotta have it
I spread my wings to fly away
But you pull my lust and make me stay.

Oh, how your warmth fills my bucket of curiosity
That didn't kill the cat
Get back
I try to get away
As your rhythm begins to sway

Back and forth, up and down
Inside out, I turn around
To stare, to get a glimpse
Of this rare feeling

To my demise, my surprise
I'm alone, again
Just me and a pen
Subtraction of love
Plus one to the end."

As usual, the crowd filled the room with applause. I was ready to go. I hoped Teresa didn't mind if we made our way back to her apartment.

"Teresa, I'm ready to go. What about you?"

"Why, because Breeze isn't here? We've only been here for an hour."

"Well, you aren't talkative. We aren't drinking and it's not even crowded tonight."

"You don't have to justify why you want to leave. I know it's because Breeze isn't here," Teresa said sarcastically.

I looked at Teresa without saying a word.

"Come on. We can go have our own party at my apartment," she said.

After Joi's, we headed back to Teresa's apartment.

Pouring a drink Teresa said, "Beauty, I wasn't about to spend all that money on drinks when I can get toasted at the house."

I shook my head in disbelief.

"Let's toast to our girls' night out," she said.

Before I knew it, we were sloppy drunk. We talked about the first time we both had sex, our fears, and our childhood dreams. Teresa said when she grew up she wanted to be a criminal lawyer. I told her I wanted to be a ballerina.

"A ballerina? You have no rhythm!"

"Forget you, Teresa. It's better than your profession!"

"Oh yeah? How?" She asked, stammering over her words.

I paused and mumbled, "I guess you would be a good lawyer."

We laughed.

"Teresa, you know I love you."

"What!"

"I said," stumbling over my words, "you know I love you."

"Wait. You love me. No. No. No. I love you and there is nothing you can do about it," she managed to say.

We giggled uncontrollably. The last thing I remembered, I told Teresa was about Sarai's request to have me partake in her and her husband's love affair.

The next morning I woke up with the worst headache.

"Teresa! I've gotta go," I said.

I shoved her body back and forth picking up my keys. She hummed something I didn't understand.

"Teresa, Breeze is coming to pick me up in an hour. I'm leaving!"

She sluggishly raised her hand and waved goodbye.

While I was driving home, my phone beeped. I didn't read it until I arrived home.

"Just wanted to say we are goin' 2 chu'ch! LOL! I'll c ya @ 10:30a,"
Breeze's text message read.

Church? I couldn't remember the last time I went to church. Maybe this church thing could work. Maybe it would create a new chapter in my life. I walked to my closet and stared at my wardrobe. *I could wear a pantsuit.*

No. I'm not sure if people wear pants to Breeze's church. Maybe I'll wear this beige dress. Nope. That wouldn't work either. I need to look beautiful and sexy. Wait, can I be sexy and go to church? Oh, this is too difficult, he'll be here soon. Randy is probably turning over in his grave. He tried to get me to go to Ms. Henderson's church, but I never agreed.

I took some medicine to get rid of my headache. After that, I took a quick shower and decided to wear a simple black dress. I applied my makeup succinctly with the curve of my lips and layered eye shadow. My mascara extended the length of my eyelashes. *There, I'm ready.*

There was a knock at the door. Breeze was the first man after Randy's death I'd allow to come to my home.

"Who is it?"

"It's Breeze."

I waited a minute to calm my nerves. I unlocked the locks and opened the door. There he stood: tall, dark, and handsome, displaying his beautiful teeth and dimple.

"Hi Breeze."

"Good morning," he said as he extended a bouquet of mixed flowers.

"Thank you. These flowers are beautiful."

I grabbed the flowers and offered him a seat.

"Let me put these flowers in some water."

I searched for a vase. I didn't have time to prune the flowers. I went into the bedroom, put on my shoes, and grabbed my purse. I sprayed on some perfume Sarai bought me last week.

"You smell heavenly," Breeze said.

"Good. Then I won't have a problem going to heaven."

He shook his head and grabbed my hand. I turned back to lock the door. I locked away my old life, and was ready to unlock the doors to a new one.

CHAPTER TWELVE

B reeze and I talked the all the way to church. He told me all about his quest as an upcoming talk show host. He also mentioned he was close to his mother, that he didn't have any children and was never married.

"And no, I'm not gay, bisexual, or on the down low," Breeze said.

"What!"

Breeze caught me off guard.

"Where did that come from?"

"I don't know. I feel I had to make it known. Women always assume because a brother is not married, with no kids and no steady girlfriend, that he's gay."

We arrived at his church a few minutes later.

"I got it," he said as he opened my door, gallantly grabbing my hand and helping me out the car.

We walked up the stairs to the church. I noticed an ATM inside the lobby.

"An ATM inside the church? Really?" I said, pointing like a little kid at Disneyland.

"Hey that machine comes in handy."

I thought it was somewhat odd, but I didn't want to judge a book by its cover.

"Beauty! Beauty Marie Summers!"

I released Breeze's hand and turned around.

"Aunt Elizabeth?"

She looked more beautiful than ever. Her dainty navy blue and white polka dot dress complimented her complexion. She wore white gloves to accentuate her white hat. The last time I saw Aunt Elizabeth was when she came a week after Randy's funeral to collect all of his belongings.

We hugged as if we hadn't seen each other in years, although, it was now three months since Randy's funeral. I kissed her on the cheek and hugged her again. Seeing Aunt Elizabeth made me think of Randy. I felt guilty gazing at Breeze.

"Owen. I didn't know you knew my sweet darling Beauty," she said as she pushed my hair away from my face and cupped my cheek with her hand.

I forgot Owen was Breeze's real name. I was used to calling him Breeze.

"Yes, ma'am. I feel as though I've known Beauty for quite some time," Breeze said as he rubbed my back.

I thought Aunt Elizabeth was going to mention Randy.

"Well, just take good care of her Owen. She deserves nothing but the best," she said.

Aunt Elizabeth hugged me again.

"I love you Beauty. Now, I've gotta go get my praise on! I hope you enjoy the service," she said as she raised her hands up in the air.

"Sister Henderson can sing," Breeze said.

"Yes, I know."

I thought about the song she beautifully harmonized at Randy's funeral.

"Is everything OK?" Breeze asked.

Snapping out of my thoughts I replied, "I'm fine."

76

"Good. Let's enjoy life and take it one day at a time," he said.

The ushers extended their hands, smiling and gesturing for us to walk in. I followed Breeze into the sanctuary.

The choir soothingly sang:

> "I'm in need of a blessing Lord.
> I'm in need of a miracle.
> I'm in need of a blessing Lord.
> I'm in need of a miracle.
> Thank you Lord for blessing me
> I'm in need of a miracle.
> Thank you Lord for setting me free,
> For I'm in need of a miracle."

"As you can see, our church can be laid back. You know the Bible says to come as you are," Breeze said, leaning toward my ear.

Breeze must have read my mind, or either my blank stare gave my thoughts away. Everyone appeared to be friendly. People approached me and welcomed me to the church. Some shook my hand and introduced themselves, some smiled, and others gave me a hug. I didn't know church could be full of warmth and inviting. We sat in the middle of the sanctuary. The picture of Jesus behind the choir looked as if he was staring at me. Feeling as though He spoke to my soul, I shuffled from side to side.

"Are you comfortable here? We can sit toward the back," Breeze said.

"No. I'm fine. I'm just a little cold."

I couldn't believe I lied in church. Convicted of my thoughts, I stood next to Breeze attempting to sing along with the choir. Time didn't pass too long before the minister stood up to give a sermon.

"Now if you turn with me to Isaiah 30:18. Please stand if you are able to," the minister said.

I read the scripture projected on the overhead screen. The minister eloquently read the passage with passion. I became fixated on his title of the sermon—God of Grace, God of Mercy. Standing next to Breeze made me feel like my life was ready for a change.

After the reading of the scripture I sat nestled next to Breeze. I keyed in to every word the minister said. It felt as if he spoke directly to me.

"Don't settle for something that makes you feel comfortable but isn't true. It's much better to face reality than to live a lie. Consult God. By reading His word and actively seeking to do His will, we can maintain our bond with Him, who provides stability, no matter what the crisis is. We can trust Him and be peacefully confident that He will give us strength to face our difficulties. We should lay aside our busy cares and endless efforts, and allow Him to act. When we hear His voice of correction, we must be willing to follow it," the minister said.

"Amen!" A woman jumped up and shouted.

She yelled extremely hard that her hat wobbled as she pointed her finger toward the minister.

"You better preach," another person exclaimed.

"Let the doors of the church open," the minister said as he reached toward the congregation.

I looked back at the doors, but they were already open. I didn't want to ask Breeze what the minister meant.

"Don't be a slave to sin, which leads to death and destruction. Obey God's Word, which leads to righteous living," the minister said.

"Beauty," Breeze whispered as he interrupted my thoughts. "How are you enjoying the service?"

"I absolutely love it."

"Great. Wait until you see the poetry presentation," he said.

The minister continued, "Come and join this church. Give your life to God. Join this church, where it's not just church. It's an adventure."

After he offered the people to join the church, I asked Breeze to walk with me down the aisle. Aunt Elizabeth came and grabbed my other arm. At that moment, I knew I made a life-changing decision.

"Beauty, you are making the best decision you will ever make in your whole entire life," Aunt Elizabeth softly spoke.

My heart raced like I had ran a marathon. The minister introduced me to the congregation. Minutes later I was back in my seat. I felt different, as if all my problems vanished into Heaven.

Before the service ended, a young woman who wore a beautiful brown dress with small polka dots stood upfront. *I need to get me a polka dot dress.*

"Good morning, church," the young lady said.

"Good morning," the congregation replied.

"On behalf of the writing club, I am presenting my poem 'Just Passing By'."

She grabbed the microphone and stood in the center of the church, for all to see.

"Hey you! No you!
No, the person next to you my dear.
Can I talk to you for a minute? A second?
'Cause death has no listening ear.

I'm just softly passing by,
On my way to sweet glory,
I have a little something, something for you!
You guessed it. A short little story.

OK, last Friday,
I made a left,

SHAR STURGES

I kept on doing what I wanted to.
Fooled around, and met death.

I knew I had it going on
As far I could see
Didn't know my time was up
Mr. Lucifer was watching me.

I just had my baby,
God blessed me with a son,
But I wasn't quite focused,
I just had to have my fun!

My baby's daddy was fine
Sweet Lord, from head to toe
Dang, I knew he was no good,
But I couldn't let him go.

I'm chilling with my man,
Told my momma I'll be home late,
Gotta kick it with him, (you know)
Hmmmm—But that's when I met fate.

My mom be trippin'
I can't stand her sometimes
But boy oh boy!
If I could just take the time to rewind.

She said 'He ain't no good!
I saw him flirting with Ms. Lady,

DON'T CRY FOR LOVE

He ain't nothing
Just plain ole shady!'

Man, I knew he was cheating
But I loved him so,
I guess I didn't see it coming,
That big tag on my toe.

That Sunday it hit me,
God spoke to my heart,
He softly told me,
Baby girl, it's time for a new start.

I jumped up
Joined church right away
From that day forward
My soul had been saved."

"Hallelujah," the woman in the wobbling hat said.
The young lady continued,

"I left my baby's daddy
He didn't want to let me go
I guess he couldn't understand
Understand that I needed to grow.

That Friday night,
I was out with my homegirls,
Clubbing and creeping
Trying to be on top of the world

SHAR STURGES

I was talking to this guy
And who did I see?
It was my baby's daddy,
Staring all over me.

Before I could speak,
I felt this sharp pain,
It was too unbelievably true,
A silver bullet with no name.

I guess there was some beef,
That happened before I arrived,
Some guy tried to shoot my baby's daddy,
But I was blocking that drive.

Why God! Why?
Why did this happen to me?
I just accepted Christ.
It wasn't time to leave.

I guess I won't be able
To see my preacher do his dance,
Guess I won't see my son,
Grow to be a God-fearing man!

But it's not too late for you
To worship God all you can
I lost my chance,
You have to take a stand

Make sure you take control
Don't let situations control you
Give your all to God,
Keep it real and be true.

We'll now I've gotta go
On my way to glory
Hopefully you got something, something
From this short little story."

Everyone stood up and applauded the young woman as she walked toward her seat.

The sun shined brightly as we walked to the car. Breeze opened the car door, and we pulled out of the parking lot as the church members waved goodbye.

"What did you think of Diane's poem?" Breeze asked.

"It was phenomenal. She should recite the poem at Joi's. I've never heard of a church that had a writing club."

"Yeah. I'll tell her about Joi's. You know, our motto at church is "our church is not just any church,' " Breeze said.

"It's an adventure," we said in unison.

"I'm glad you liked my church enough to join. I guess we will go to chu'ch together, if you don't mind."

"I don't mind."

"I'm also glad we met," Breeze said as he grabbed my hand.

I felt lost in Breeze's world and I could live there forever.

"Where are we headed now?" I asked.

"Back to your place."

"My place?"

"Well, don't you want to change for our next excursion?"

My guard went up immediately. I mean, I liked Breeze a lot, but I was not ready for whatever he was about to try, at least not yet.

"Don't worry. I'll wait in the car. I'm not trying to ease my way into your home. If I wanted to try anything, wouldn't I have tried when I picked you up?" he asked.

Was Breeze a mind reader? I completely forgot I already let him in my apartment earlier.

I looked at Breeze without saying a word.

"After you change, I want to stop by my house I can change, too. It's your choice to come in or stay in the car. I want you to feel comfortable," he said.

I snickered.

"What's funny?" Breeze asked slightly laughing.

"Oh nothing."

I laughed because Breeze made me giggly.

CHAPTER THIRTEEN

The ride from my house to Breeze's was rather short. After he changed, we stopped at a local restaurant and grabbed a bite to eat. Breeze's conversation was invigorating. I was engaged in every story and every profound thought. He mentioned he graduated from Howard University. Again, I briefly thought of Howard Tendell. Within seconds I was mesmerized by Breeze's college days.

"It sounds like you had fun in college."

"Definitely. Didn't you?" he inquired.

"Oh yes! Too much to talk about now."

We laughed as I vaguely reflected on college.

Breeze went on to tell me about how he landed his own talk show. He told me he was in the entertainment industry, and kept a close circle of friends.

"Most people gravitate to me because of my profession, but not you. I really trust you. I could spend the rest of my life with you," Breeze said.

I almost melted in my chair. I was falling hard for Breeze like rain falling from the clouds onto the ground. I told Breeze about my relationship with Randy and Howard. I told him about my first crush on Bailey. I poured out my soul. Breeze was what every woman dreamed a man should be. He was what I wanted and deserved.

"I don't want to spend a day without you," I said.

"I'm glad to hear that. Let's just take life one day at a time, and enjoy each other's company," he said before kissing my lips.

After we ate, Breeze said we were on our way to fun. I was tired and sleepy. I didn't know why, but I felt exhausted. After we traveled for over an hour, I woke up screaming.

"Beauty!" Breeze yelled.

I was breathing hard. I felt pain in my stomach again.

"Are you OK?"

"I think I had a bad dream," now realizing I was riding in the car with Breeze.

We passed a sign that read San Diego Animal Wild Kingdom Next Exit. I tried to recall the details of my dream. I vaguely remembered Randy and I were arguing in my car. Suddenly, everything went dark.

"Do you want to talk about it?" Breeze asked.

"No. Well, I mean my dream wasn't clear."

He probably thought I lied.

"I see. I know what would help you. I think you need a nice vacation. Have you ever been to the Bahamas?" Breeze asked.

My eyes lit up like I won the lottery.

"A vacation?"

"Tonight, when I get home, I'll have my assistant book us a trip to the Bahamas. I'm only suggesting the Bahamas, but if you find somewhere else you'd like to go, let me know. I'm going to whisk you away on a vacation and there's nothing you can do about it, "he said, rubbing my shoulder.

"I've never been on an airplane before," I said.

I was too embarrassed to tell Breeze I was really scared to fly.

To disguise my fear I asked, "When are we leaving?"

"In two weeks we will be in the Bahamas," Breeze said.

That moment I realized Breeze was not a figment of my imagination. He was real and attentive to my needs. A man who knew what he wanted; ambitious; creative; and a man who wanted to take care of me.

We pulled into the parking lot.

"Well, here we are," he said.

"The zoo? I haven't been to the zoo since I was a kid."

"It's not just any zoo, this is San Diego's Wild Animal Kingdom."

"Oh, please pardon me!"

We laughed.

"Today, we'll act like kids and enjoy ourselves without a care in the world," he said.

Breeze was right. This was the best zoo ever. We saw every animal I could imagine. My favorite was the ride through Safari Park. Touching the giraffes was yet another memory Breeze created in this chapter of my life. We stayed there until the zoo closed. There was loads of traffic back on the way home. I felt bad for falling asleep again. I woke up when Breeze closed the driver's side door. He opened my door, helped me out the car, and gave me a hug as he tried to get rid of all my pain. I grabbed him even tighter.

"I enjoyed our day," Breeze said.

My knees buckled, but I managed to hold myself up. I looked into his eyes and kissed him on his lips. I couldn't resist and neither could he. Breeze received my heartfelt invitation of reciprocity. Our tongues met full of lust and desire. If this were a soap opera, the music would serenade our passion. Breeze walked me to my door. I opened it and said goodbye.

"Remember, let's just take life one day at time," Breeze said with a smile.

We kissed again. I then closed and locked the door. I watched him walk away through the peephole. Afterward, I ran to my computer and quickly searched for the Bahamas. I never saw such beautiful pictures. *The Bahamas—here we come.*

CHAPTER FOURTEEN

I decided to hang out at Joi's alone, despite the absence of Breeze. I visited Joi's less since Breeze and I started dating. Thoughts of fear continued to trample in my mind when I thought about standing on stage reciting one of my poems. Nothing seemed to have changed at Joi's. Nikki was still happy-go-lucky. The same people were in the audience on Friday nights. Jenson, the DJ, was in his usual corner, with one headphone slightly pulled away from one ear. Pete, the bouncer, wore his usual Jamaican wristband, black T-shirt, and jeans.

Joi took the stage.

"All right, all right. Our next poet was showcased in our I've Got Talent Search last month. Let's welcome back Mamma J!" Joi said as the crowd applauded.

Mama J stepped on stage. Her salt and pepper hair shined in the spotlight. She froze for a moment as we listened to the stillness of air. She had one hand on her hip and her head tilted to the side. She used her other hand to shade the light as she stared at the audience. Her dress looked like a print from an old '70s sofa. She wore black stockings and black shoes with thick rubber soles. She dropped her hands and told her story:

"Come here
Gather around and listen

SHAR STURGES

As I attempt to bestow
Knowledge that you may be missin'

A black woman made to do it all
Ha! You may say
Well, let's have some small talk
Oh, and I don't need no privacy

As a black woman
My back was often scared
I was told I was ugly
And was forced to slave in the yard

We were even divided
Amongst ourselves
The lighter of me slaved indoors
Getting in good with Mr. Wealth

The darker me had to endure
All that darn heat
And was dared to roll my eyes
And forbidden to suck my teeth

Let me tell you about the black woman
Who was made to do it all
Why we had to scrub the floors
Cook the food, wash the clothes, and yes wash the walls

Half the time
I was too tired to even speak

DON'T CRY FOR LOVE

To my strong black brother
Whom they loved to beat."

The crowd was silent as they listened to every word, every symbol, and followed every movement Mama J made.

"Walking around barefoot
On those hard wooden floors
Praying through the seasons
As my feet sprouted sores

A black woman
Made to do it all
Why I can hold 10 items at once
Without letting anything fall

Do you perhaps know why
The black woman is strong today
Because we don't have time
To put up with your silly play
We are about business
Huh, for the most
If it ain't broke,
Don't fix it. Just relax and let it flow

Thank you, Lord,
For creating me from sand
A strong blessed intellectual
Destined to be the rib of a black man

God created us
In his own image
It's like playing football
We've gotta be ready on the line of scrimmage

Trust in the Lord
With all your heart
Keep on pressing
Toward the mark

A black woman made to do it all
Don't fear! Don't fret
Because I am black woman, made to do it all
And I will earn my due respect."

Everyone raised their hands in the air and snapped their fingers, while others applauded. I wish Sarai were here. She would've loved Mamma J. My phone vibrated. It was Sarai. How ironic. She sent me a text message:

"Beauty where r u? We need to talk."

My heart dropped to the floor. I hope she didn't find out about Doug and me. I didn't mean for it to happen. Guilt settled in my thoughts like a cheater caught in the act. I reluctantly replied:

"I'll be over soon."

Sarai quickly replied:

"Come over as soon as you can."

My remorse immediately subsided, but I hoped Sarai was OK. I was ready to leave Joi's anyway. Nikki came to my table and sat with me. She told me that she wanted me to be a featured poet next month. I laughed at the idea.

"Nikki, you know how terrified I am. I have a serious case of stage fright."

"Would it help if Breeze was here?" She said jokingly as she pushed me with her shoulder.

"Breeze or no Breeze. Uh uh. I'm not doing it!"

"Joi was looking for some new talent for next month and I told her all about you."

"I'm sorry Nikki. I just can't do it. Not now."

"Well if not now, then when? Beauty you have talent. Just think about it," she said as she scooted back her chair.

Before Nikki could pick up her tray, a man seated at the next table motioned to get her attention. She gestured back to him that she was on her way.

"I've read some of your poems Beauty, remember? I don't want you to be a woulda, shoulda, coulda. Life's too short."

Without waiting for a response, Nikki walked away. The ball was in my court, but at that moment, I wanted to let it go out of bounds.

CHAPTER FIFTEEN

On the way home, I couldn't stop thinking about my fear of performing on stage. I remembered as a child I would get the stepladder and stand on top. My dad would listen to me read my poems. However, I was too shy to stand in front of a crowd. I remember when Ms. Taten, my 10th grade English teacher, asked for volunteers to read poems we wrote from last night's homework assignment. At the sight of no raised hands and rambunctious children who giggled among themselves, Ms. Taten summoned me from the class. I guess I was a target because I was busy daydreaming. I walked to the front of the room as my classmates oohed and ahhed. My hands began to shake as I held the paper up front. I couldn't read past the title.

"Let me see, Beauty," Ms. Taten said.

Ms. Taten gently pulled the paper from my frozen hands.

"The Flameless Soul," she read.

The class fell silent. Ms. Taten continued to read.

> "The fire is burning with painful memories
> Of one's vast relationship
> Trust is unheard of
> And hate is purely fed
> One wishes to wake up from this dream

But a dream it is not
Reality it must be
Reconciliation is made
But the true fire never ceases
It still burns in the heart and soul."

Everyone clapped. When I walked back to my seat, many of my classmates raised their hands to receive high-fives.

"Beauty, you have no reason to be shy. That poem was absolutely fabulous. Make sure you remember me when you become a famous poet," Ms. Taten said.

Ms. Taten had no idea I was afraid to speak in front of a crowd.

I rung Sarai's doorbell. She didn't answer. I faintly heard her crying.

"Sarai, is that you? It's Beauty. Open the door!"

There was still no answer. Frantically I went home. I remembered Sarai gave me a spare key in case of an emergency. I never thought I would ever have to use it. *I have no idea where I put that key.* I rushed and opened my front door. I ran to my bedroom, opened one of my dresser drawers, and threw my underwear on the bed. The key wasn't there. I ran to the kitchen and checked another drawer. *Nothing.*

I grabbed my cell phone and tried to call Sarai. She didn't answer. When I went back to my bedroom I saw the key on my nightstand.

How did that get there? Without having time to ponder, I ran back to Sarai's apartment. *Damn!* I realized I left my keys on the bed and I was now locked out of my apartment.

I fumbled Sarai's spare key into the lock.

"Sarai. Where are you?"

The crying became louder and louder. I followed the whimpering and found Sarai seated on the floor holding a picture frame.

"What's wrong? What's going on?"

Without waiting for a response, I sat down next to Sarai. She grabbed me and sobbed uncontrollably.

"Doug left me! Doug left me!" She said.

"What? I don't understand?"

"My husband left me!" She yelled in desperation.

For the first time in my life, I didn't know what to say or do. Sarai laid on the floor in a fetal position. I didn't have the courage to ask her what happened. I pulled the blanket down from the bed and covered her. I went to the bathroom and grabbed a roll of tissue, and placed the tissue next to Sarai's head.

"Everything will be OK, Sarai. You'll see."

She stared blankly at me as my words fell on the floor and shattered.

I sat next to Sarai and comforted her with soft rubs on her arm, like a mother trying to soothe a crying baby. She continued to hug the picture frame. I managed to get a peek. It was a picture Sarai and Doug took on their wedding day.

The next morning, I woke up with a stiff neck. Sarai was asleep. The frame, still in her hand, rested slightly on the floor. I tiptoed out of the bedroom and quietly walked through the living room to the kitchen. I wanted to leave Sarai a note. I searched for a piece of paper and pen. I noticed a letter on the counter from a Dr. Katz. The letter disclosed some results and indicated Sarai was not able to have children. I knew she wanted to start a family, but often blamed Doug as a reason for their infertility. *This couldn't be a reason for Doug to leave Sarai.* Baffled, I moved the letter over and wrote on the torn envelope:

Please call me
X Beauty

I placed the envelope near the frame Sarai was holding. I closed the door and then remembered I didn't have my key to get into my apartment. I went to the leasing office and asked the receptionist if someone could let me in. I was still wearing my clothes from last night. My hair was uncombed, but I didn't care. The receptionist said she would alert Mr. Bill, the maintenance man. I always tried to avoid Mr. Bill as much as possible. He constantly complained about life, politics, and religion. He never had anything positive to say.

"You locked yourself out? Now how on Earth did you manage to do that?" Mr. Bill asked as he jingled his keys.

Before I could answer, he continued his conversation.

"You know everybody is trying to keep me down," we said in unison.

He stopped in his tracks and looked at me. Mr. Bill expressed that statement frequently. The elevator ride up to my apartment appeared drastically long. I didn't provide any insight to his conversation, and pretended to listen attentively. He finally opened my door. I thanked Mr. Bill as he mumbled himself back to the elevator.

I checked my phone. I had several missed calls: a couple from Breeze, an unrecognized number, one blocked call, and a call from Kate. I wondered what Kate wanted. Kate and I worked together. We've known each other for years. I checked my messages. Breeze left a few messages saying he was worried since he had not heard from me.

I also had a text message from Kate that read:

"Beauty! Hey girl! I miss you over here! Call me!
I have some good jg!"

Kate always had juicy gossip or as she called it "jg." During lunch, she filled my ears with recent office affairs, love triangles, threats, and thieves. Kate left no stone unturned. She dated off and on Keaton, an executive in Sales. I sent a text to Kate to call me and then I called Breeze.

"Are you all right? I was worried," Breeze said.

"I'm sorry. Sarai sent me a text while I was at Joi's, asking if I could come over. When I arrived, she didn't answer the door. I went to grab the spare key she'd given me."

I paused. I couldn't understand how the key mysteriously appeared on my nightstand.

"Hello. Are you there? Hello? What's wrong?" Breeze anxiously asked.

"I'm here."

I didn't want to tell him about the key mysteriously appearing.

"Long story short, I locked myself out."

"I'm glad you're OK. How's Sarai?" he asked.

"Not well. She was extremely distraught. She kept murmuring, 'Doug left me.' "

I didn't go into details about the letter I read from Dr. Katz.

"What! I can't believe that! They seemed like a couple that had it all!"

"Yeah, tell me about it."

"Well, I'm glad you're OK. Do you have any plans this evening? I'll be over tonight."

"Yep. I have plans."

"Oh," Breeze said sounding disappointed.

"I plan on being with you."

"Oh ok. You've got jokes. I'll see you tonight."

Unbeknownst to me, I fell asleep on the sofa. The ringtone on my cell phone played. It was Kate. When I answered she was ecstatic. I was thrilled just as much as she was. I spent most of my time with her at work during breaks and lunches. We also hung out at Maria's Cantina on Taco Tuesdays and Margarita Fridays after work. Kate kept me on the phone for at least an hour. She told me how Josh, the cutest man in Accounting, underwent a sex change. When he came back to work after a short leave, no one recognized him.

"He was totally dressed in a skirt and cute blouse. They escorted Josh, I mean, Josephina out the building. Can you believe that? He came back to work after a threat of a lawsuit. And guess where he's sitting?" Kate questioned.

Before I could answer Kate continued, "right next to your cubicle," she said laughing. "Now you can give me some 'jg' on Josh, I mean Josephina."

"That's exactly what I was thinking."

We laughed like two true friends who enjoyed each other's company. Kate went on to tell me how much she missed having breaks and lunches with me; but she especially missed our trips to Maria's Cantina. She expressed her condolences regarding Randy, even though he passed four months ago. I knew she couldn't make it to the funeral, because she and Keaton had already planned a weekend getaway. She told me she missed reading my poems and hearing about my crazy friends. I didn't mention Sarai's new ordeal.

Kate went on to talk about Ned, our supervisor.

"You know he corrects everything I write. I'm not talking about grammatical errors. I'm talking about simple words or complete paragraph changes. Like last week. I referred to the word 'employee' in a memo . . . Get this, Beauty. He told me to change every reference of 'employee' to 'staff'," she said.

"You've got to be kidding me."

"Nope. I asked Ned what the difference was, and he said 'staff' sounds more professional."

"Don't worry about it. You'll have his position soon."

"He makes me feel as if I need to take remedial English," Kate replied.

"Well, you know that's not the case, otherwise you wouldn't have a master's degree. Have you told Ned how you feel?"

"No. He's tremendously irritating. Every time he walks by he's staring at my screen. I've even caught him peeping around the corner to see if I'm at my desk, not wanting a thing. I don't how much more I can take."

"Hang in there. I'll be back before you know it and then we can sabotage Ned together! I just need some personal time off from work, since Randy's death."

"I know, but I'm thinking about leaving the company."

"No! If you leave before I return, my life will be boring in that place without you."

"How do you think I feel now?" She asked.

"Point taken."

"I'm thinking about not dating Keaton anymore. Jackson in Legal keeps dropping subtle hints that he wants to go out," she said.

"Jackson? In Legal? Wow. Every single woman will be jealous."

Laughing, Kate told me there was a man in her section who recently inquired about me. She refused to tell me who and said I had to wait until I came back to work to find out who the mysterious man was. I didn't tell her about Breeze. I didn't want to seem like I was on the rebound quickly after Randy's death. Thirty minutes later, we finished our conversation and hung up the phone as two satisfied gossipers on the horizon again.

CHAPTER SIXTEEN

Today was the first Saturday in a long time that I decided to stay home and do nothing. I remembered when my dad always made sure I had something to do on Saturdays. Like the time he had Mrs. Capshaw, who lived down the street, take me to the skating ring, the Skate Factory, every Saturday morning. Mrs. Capshaw was Tyla's adopted parent. Tyla was my neighborhood friend, but we weren't as close as my other friend Althea. Mr. Capshaw was always at work. I rarely saw him on Saturdays or any other day. Tyla was very spoiled. She had everything a girl could ever want: her own room, two bikes, and the newest fashions. Although my dad could afford to buy me anything I wanted, he believed I had to do chores.

"Save your money and I will help you get what you want. Saving money builds character," my dad said constantly.

Charity would sneak and give me a one hundred dollar bill every now and again. I was very thankful. She said it was our little secret.

One Saturday Mrs. Capshaw told me, "Beauty, this Saturday, you gonna learn how to skat."

Mrs. Capshaw had a heavy Southern drawl. I barely understand her at times.

"I'm sorry Mrs. Capshaw, what did you say?"

"I best believe you need your ears checked, Beauty. I said, today you gonna learn how to skat . . . skat," she said again.

Tyla leaned over and whispered in my ear to tell me her mom said I was going to learn how to skate. We both giggled as Mrs. Capshaw shook her head.

"I don't know what I'm gonna do with the both of you," she said.

When we arrived at The Skate Factory, Althea and her brother Bailey were there too. Althea, Tyla, and I sat at the benches noticing every young boy at The Skate Factory while eating a slice of pepperoni pizza. I couldn't tell Tyla or Althea that I had a huge crush on her brother.

"Come on Beauty, they are starting a skating line," Althea said as she and Tyla stood up.

I didn't move.

"You know I can't skate like that," I said.

"All you have to do is hold on to my waist and I'll guide you," Tyla said.

Both Tyla and Althea took my hands. I slowly moved down the ramp onto the floor. As the DJ played "Freaks Come Out at Night" by Whodini, everyone skated in a circle as they held on to the waist of the person in front of them. Althea's brother was the best skater there. He broke out of the ring and went into the middle of the circle. He skated backwards, sideways, and added a few handstands in between. I was completely mesmerized by Bailey's skating. I forgot what I was doing, lost control, and fell. Before I knew it, Althea, Tyla, and several other people fell to the ground too. I was embarrassed and wanted to leave. Bailey skated to me and helped me up. He took me by the hand and showed me a few skating tricks. My embarrassment went away. One thing was for sure, Mrs. Capshaw was right. I did learn to "skat" that day.

Suddenly there was a knock at my door. I looked through the peephole. I didn't see anyone. An envelope slid under my door. On the outside it read: YOU SHOULD KNOW. I opened the door and looked down the hallway. There was no one in sight. I closed the door and picked up the letter-sized manila envelope. I sat on the sofa and opened it. I couldn't believe my eyes. There were pictures of Randy with another man, hugging and kissing. In one picture, Randy raised his hand to cover his face, but whoever it was still took the picture. I stood up in awe and disgust. *I know this is not what I think it is. How could he do this to me?* I immediately felt cramps in my stomach. The pain was too hard to bear. Seconds later, I passed out.

There was a knock at the door. I jumped up from the couch. I looked around. There was no envelope. Was this déjà vu? The knock became louder.

"Beauty! It's Sarai!"

Baffled by the dream I just had, I yelled back, "OK, I'm on my way!"

I opened the door. Sarai looked like she had lost weight. We hadn't talked since the last time I left her apartment a couple of weeks ago.

"Come in."

She sat on the sofa and patted the cushion to gesture for me to sit next to her. Sarai began to talk about her years growing up in Brooklyn. She told me how she moved from one apartment to the next and how her mother was heavily on drugs. To pay for her mother's drug habits, her mother would make her have sex with the drug dealers. She said that after she turned sixteen, she told her mother she didn't want to live that kind of lifestyle anymore. Her mother didn't want to put up with it, so she kicked Sarai out on the streets. Sarai eventually turned to prostitution to survive.

"I met Ms. Weathers at the abortion clinic. She told me there was a way out. She gave me information of a shelter that helped women get off the streets," Sarai said.

"I'm sorry you had to go through that."

"Yeah. Well I was there for my 10th abortion. I knew something needed to change."

I was stunned. I'd never imagine she'd have this story to share.

"Ms. Weathers told me I couldn't use abortion like it was a contraceptive and could possibly end up not being able to conceive when I was ready."

She went on to say that she didn't stay at the shelter for long. She said she returned to her life on the streets.

"One day, my pimp beat me bad when I became pregnant again. I didn't know who the father was. The situation escalated when I told him I was keeping the baby. He became enraged, pulled out his gun, and pistol-whipped me. He dropped me off at the abortion clinic. Ms. Weathers was there that day and rushed me to the hospital. I had a miscarriage."

She said Ms. Weathers didn't give up on her, although, after she left the hospital she went back to her pimp.

"When I went back to the abortion clinic for my thirteenth abortion, Ms. Weathers practically yelled at me. She asked why I didn't go to the shelter or let alone take the birth control pills she gave me? She kept saying over and over, abortion was not a form of birth control!"

Sarai said that day was a revelation. After her conversation with Ms. Weathers, she took a cab to a shelter. She said she stayed there for almost a year. She started working a part-time job at a local fitness center, where she met Doug. He was in town for basketball training. Eventually the two became engaged and moved to Los Angeles. Sarai said she and Doug tried to have a baby for over three years before she decided to go to the doctor.

Teary-eyed she said, "That's when I found out I had too many abortions. They completely damaged my uterus. I can't have children."

She said Doug didn't know about her past life, and she never told him about the abortions. When he found out, he couldn't believe she would do such a thing.

"I tried to plead with Doug that my past was in the past. I told him I am a different woman now, but he wouldn't listen. That's when he told me he was leaving me for another woman."

My guilt was a tasteless bud on my tongue. I attempted to swallow my feelings away.

"Doug told me what happened between the two of you," she said.

Dumbfounded, I couldn't find the words to explain.

"Don't bother explaining. Believe me, you aren't the first, and you weren't the last," she said.

I slouched down, like a puppy that was sorry for chewing on his owner's favorite shoe.

"Beauty, you have been there for me in many ways. I'm glad you moved next door. I know I should probably be mad at you, but women have to stick together. Thank you for coming over to console me. I'm sorry I didn't get back to you. I didn't know what to do with myself."

"I-," she wouldn't let me interrupt.

"I've admired how you kept hanging in there with Randy. I can honestly say he didn't deserve you. I'm glad you are with Breeze now. I'm moving to Chicago in a few days. I just wanted to say good-bye," she said sadly.

We both stood up and gave each other a hug. I told Sarai how sorry I was about Doug and I really would miss her friendship.

"Now who's going to hang out with me at Joi's?" I asked sobbing.

We hugged again and cried.

Before Sarai opened the door, she said, "You have to get some guts and get on that stage. The world is waiting on you."

She spoke with her eyes as if they were the windows to her soul. She reached over and kissed me on the cheek like a sister who was leaving for college. I closed the door and wondered how to tell the world that I was ready. Ready to conquer my fears, ready to give them what I had all along—the love and joy of poetry.

Have you ever wondered
What someone else's eyes have seen?
While either they were awake
Or shuffling in their nocturnal dream?

I do, I wonder
What lies were told
Or what choices they made
To get them down their current road

It's interesting to think
What someone's focus has become
Did they always see clear?
Or was their vision perished or numbed

If I could look
Just once through your soul
What would it say to me?
What would unfold?

Perhaps some untold miseries
Or dreams left behind

DON'T CRY FOR LOVE

No one will ever know
Unless the bow was untied

What have your eyes truly seen?
What may the truth be?
Pondering through your eyes
What would they reveal to me?

CHAPTER SEVENTEEN

The moment Sarai left, Teresa called. She told me that she had something to tell me. *What was this, confession day?* Everyone wanted to open up to me and tell me all their dark secrets. If they only knew I had tons of skeletons in my own closet. In fact, some of the skeletons complained how crowded it was and moved to another one; two closets, full of skeletons, with only one life to live.

"Why don't you tell me what's going on? Why do I have to wait until you get here?"

Teresa said she was on her way and she would tell me everything when she arrived. I decided to take a shower. I almost loathed showering. Randy's words played repeatedly in my mind, "Why did you do it, Beauty?" My showers became shorter and shorter by the day. Afterward, I decided to take a quick nap. I was exhausted even though I hadn't done much of anything. I closed my eyes as my thoughts wandered away.

The clock read 4:57 a.m. and Randy was still not home. I tried to go back to sleep but couldn't. I decided to get up and write. When I wrote, I focused less on Randy's whereabouts. I searched for my writing tablet and realized I'd left it in the car. I put my slippers on and grabbed my coat. I took the elevator down to the underground parking garage. I saw Randy sitting in his car, talking on his cell phone. I froze completely. He leaned his head back as he laughed. I ducked between cars, swiftly approached the driver's side, and knocked as hard as I could on the window. Startled, Randy jumped and dropped the phone. He opened the car door. His car keys fell to the ground. He leaned down to grab them. I wanted to push him down to the ground.

"Who are you talking to at this time in the morning?"

"Hey, I was just thinking of you," he said, trying to change the subject.

"Please. Spare me."

I threw my hands up in the air.

"I don't have time for your lies. Who were you talking to? And when did you get a new cell phone?"

"Whoa, whoa, whoa. I wasn't talking on the phone. I was looking at the features. I found it," he said as he stuffed the black phone into his back pocket.

I stood there with my arms folded, not giving in to my devious plots to hurt him.

"What's with these twenty questions, anyway?" Randy asked.

I resisted the urge to kick him right between his legs. The vision of him kneeling over, falling to the ground in pain, made me smile. I blinked and came back to reality. Walking toward the building, he called my name, but I ignored him. I went back to the apartment and locked all the doors.

I forgot to get my tablet. I hit my hand against my forehead and kicked my shoes off. One landed on top of the dresser, knocking down my perfume. I didn't bother to remove it. I threw Randy's pillow on the floor and pulled all the covers from Randy's side of the bed over to mine.

"Beauty, why did you lock the door? You knew I was coming in. What's wrong with you?"

"What's wrong with me? Whatever."

I took the extra pillow and threw it at him. From that moment, I knew something had to change. He picked up the pillow and threw it back, laughing.

"I'm not playing with you. I'm tired of your lies!" I shouted.

"Beauty, I know you are not playing with me. Wake up!" Teresa said as she threw the pillow at me. Startled, I jumped that I nearly fell off the sofa.

"How did you get in?"

"You left your door unlocked. I knocked and knocked. You didn't answer. When I turned the knob, the door opened."

"Oh. Sarai left not too long ago to tell me she's moving to Chicago. I guess I forgot to lock it. I'm glad it was you and not someone else."

"Well, what time is Breeze coming to pick us up to go to Joi's?"

I looked at the clock.

"He's on his way!"

I couldn't believe I had slept for over two hours.

While we were at Joi's, Teresa was very quiet. When Breeze went to the restroom, I didn't wait another minute to find out Teresa's confession.

"You said you had something to tell me?"

"I'll tell you later. Not here."

"Forget it then."

"OK. OK. On my way to your house, there was too much traffic. I couldn't figure out why. You won't believe what happened."

Clearly Teresa evaded the question.

"Now you're being funny."

"No I'm not. Guess what happened?" Teresa asked.

"What?"

"There was a man who pushed a fruit cart in the middle of the street. I guess he tried to beat the traffic. Midway across the street, his fruit cart fell over," she said laughing.

I tried not to giggle, but her laughter was contagious.

"The sad part about it is that no one stopped to help the man pick up the fruit."

She laughed even harder. Before I could make another comment, Breeze walked on stage.

"Hey, how is everybody doing out there tonight?"

"What is Breeze doing?" Teresa asked.

Her guess was as good as mine. The silhouette of his body reflected on the wall. I undressed him repeatedly subconsciously.

"I want to dedicate this poem to my beautiful Beauty," he said, staring in my direction.

I was in total shock. No one had ever dedicated anything to me before.

He began to recite his poem. I could see the words pouring from his heart while they danced for me on the floor, on the table, and jumped into my soul. The motion of my body swayed back and forth. Our rhythm was one. Together we dangled our love in the air for the whole crowd to see.

"When our spirits meet
It's as if we've talked before
I get excited
When I see you walk through the door
You don't ever have to say a word

A simple nod will do
Because when our spirits meet
I feel fresh and renewed

DON'T CRY FOR LOVE

It's funny how I know
What you're thinking deep down inside
Most of the time you speak
But when you don't, our spirits seem to glide

I wonder if you feel it
Do you feel the way I do?
Oh, how I wish I were your husband
God knows I would be true

Sitting here weekly
Wishing I could say
Just how deeply I truly care
As our spirits soar their way

When you gently hug me
Without saying a word
My spirit seems to soar
As high as God's precious bird

I guess I'll just wait
For our kindred souls to speak
Until that time comes
Just our spirits shall continue to meet."

Breeze stepped off stage. Warped by lust, we kissed. I didn't care who was around. I kissed a man who sent a peaceful breeze in my life.

CHAPTER EIGHTTEEN

I sit and burn
Like the wick of a candle
My body melts with
The thought of your love
Addicted to your warmth
Your touch . . . your thoughts
I long for your love

Day in and day out
Sitting alone once again
This pain digs deep
I can't let go
I feel the waters of love

When will we be one?
Wrapped in the heat of passion
I see you with my soul
Caressing my mind
Come home my love
I'm waiting endlessly
For you . . .

Come home
To a love burning . . .
Like the wick of a candle

B urning candles made me feel at ease. Especially since it had been four and a half months since Randy's death. At night I kept having dreams of receiving pictures of Randy with another man, although, I couldn't quite recall who the other man was. I then remembered having other dreams of me arguing with Randy in a car. My thoughts instantly reverted to Breeze. I couldn't figure out what was going on in my head. Maybe I should see a psychiatrist. Sigmund Freud believed all dreams have interpretations. *I wonder what my dreams are trying to illustrate.*

The time had finally arrived for Breeze and me to leave for the Bahamas. We were flying out tomorrow night. I was already packed. I searched the Internet on what to take. Exhausted and excited, I was ready to lay my head on my big fluffy pillow when there was a knock at the door. It was Teresa. She said she really wanted to talk to me . . . and not about the man whose cart fell over in the street.

I took the wet umbrella, opened it up in the kitchen to let it dry, and hung her jacket on the coat rack in the corner. She had a sad look on her face. I knew something was wrong. I remembered our last trip to Joi's. She was quiet and her attention span was short. She was not the same. She plopped down on the sofa and stared at the floor.

I pointed to the kitchen, "Would you like something to drink?"

I realized I had opened the umbrella inside. I couldn't remember who told me it was bad luck, so rushed over to close it.

"No. I really need to talk to you right now," she sighed. "Remember Satan? I mean, Eldon?"

Concerned, I sat next to Teresa on the sofa. Before she continued, I thought about the day I came over her house and she told me Sheila was expecting Eldon's baby. That was the day I thought I stole $300 from the box with the Kente cloth that was in front of Teresa's apartment.

"How could I forget?"

"I really haven't told you the whole story," she said.

Teresa went on to say how she hid the abuse Eldon took her through. She said they did break up because she got pregnant by some-one else and used that as an escape goat to kick him out. I thought about how every time I encountered Eldon he was polite. He wasn't rude or hostile.

"Beauty, there were times when we would get into a physical fight. You know I don't believe in letting a man hit me, I would definitely fight back. He would just catch me off guard sometimes," Teresa said.

"How would the fights start?"

"The first time we fought it was because he found out I cheated, which I couldn't understand, because he cheated first."

I wanted to give my two cents, but something made me keep my mouth shut.

"Remember about six months ago, you said you saw a bump on my head? I told you I didn't know how it happened. Well I did. Another time I had a black eye, and I told you that it occurred while playing with my cousins? That was a lie."

Teresa went on to say that Eldon would get jealous of the "drops" Teresa made for my dad. She said Eldon swore up and down that she had a fling with my dad, which didn't make sense since my dad was in jail. Not to mention, Teresa was like my dad's adopted daughter.

"Did you tell my dad?"

"Are you kidding? You know Eldon wouldn't be alive if I did."

Teresa said the abuse took a turn when Eldon started doing drugs. He would accuse Teresa of having sex with different men. She said he would blame me sometimes and said that I had helped her meet them. I never thought Teresa would go through something like this. She had a tough persona. She was a fighter.

She continued her gruesome details of Eldon's chaotic plots and schemes.

"I swear, if I ever see him again. I swear I'll kill him!" She exclaimed.

I could see the hatred in Teresa's eyes as she relived every moment. The more she talked about Eldon, the more it made Randy seem like a saint. I had to do something to change the subject.

"Would you like to go to a party with me tonight? It starts at 8:00, but we can get there later if you'd like."

She gave in to my ploy.

"Are you going to pick me up or do you want me to come back over here?"

"I'll come get you."

Kate from work had invited me to an upcoming artist's listening party. She always had invites to celebrity parties. Most of the time I went with her. I remember one year Kate and I took a road trip to San Francisco to visit her mom, who had a few invites to an exquisite celebrity party. It was nice to travel through other parts of California. We visited Alcatraz. It made me think about how my dad lived his life incarcerated. My dad often said, "In jail is where you learn to become a better top-notch criminal. You can learn to perfect what you do best: crime." I never wanted to find out if his theory was true.

Driving over the Golden Gate Bridge was neat. I tried to curtail my thoughts of the bridge caving in, but Kate reassured me that the bridge was secure. I hoped I could suppress my negative thoughts about flying tomorrow night. *Look who's enjoying their life now, Randy?*

"Hunh?" Perplexed Teresa questioned.

For a brief moment, I forgot she was sitting there as I spoke sarcasm to Randy's listening soul.

"Oh. Sorry."

I explained the weird things that were happening around the apartment after Randy's death. She said I really needed to take a vacation with Breeze. Shortly after Teresa left, I decided to go check on Sarai. When I saw Sarai on the way to the parking lot yesterday, she said she was leaving next Tuesday. Before closing my apartment door, I made sure I had my key. When I approached Sarai's door, there was complete silence. I didn't hear any music or movement, which was odd. Sarai always left the radio on. I noticed the door was slightly opened. I slowly pushed the door.

"Sarai?"

There was no answer. Everything that belonged to Sarai and Doug was gone. No lint on the carpet, no nail holes on the wall where the picture hung of a man who sat at a grand piano with a cigar hanging in his mouth.

I walked through the apartment and called Sarai's name, even though the apartment was empty. The sound of sorrow smoothly whispered in my ear. I walked in the bedroom. On the floor I saw the photo Sarai held tightly the night she told me Doug left. Only this time the glass was shattered into tiny pieces. I walked to the window that bared the parking structure.

The day was gloomy. Dark clouds covered the sky. Who says it never rains in Southern California? I saw a bird perched on a branch, staring at me as if he could recount every last thing that happened in Sarai's apartment. I looked in the other direction outside the window and saw a couple walking to their car, hand in hand. All of my past hurts, Sarai's despair, Teresa's anger, and Randy's death . . . flowed through my tears. Drop by drop my heart weighed a ton. I walked back through the apartment and out the door, closing the doors to a past that haunted us all. Emotionally exhausted, I went home and crawled in my bed. I closed my eyes and said a prayer asking God to heal us all.

CHAPTER NINETEEN

My cell phone rang.

"Hey baby girl." It was my dad.

"How are you calling me directly? Are you home?"

"No. I have a cell phone. Store my number in your phone, you can call me anytime."

"Hunh, a cell phone? I'm not going to even ask."

"Good, because I'm not going to tell."

We laughed.

"What's going on? How are you doing?" He continued.

"I'm fine. Sarai and Doug separated, so Sarai moved out."

"Oh yeah. I know you told me you liked to hang out at Joi's with Sarai."

"Yeah. Teresa had major problems with Satan."

"With who?" He asked.

"I mean with Eldon. Dad, she told me he beat her!"

"What! No. No. Not Teresa! I definitely will make sure the situation is taken care of."

I knew that meant trouble.

"Well, I was calling to check in on my baby girl. They told me today I am going to get an early release. I'll be out next week."

"Great, I can't wait to see you. Oh, wait. I won't be in town."

I wanted to take back my every word. I was excited when I thought I was going to be out of town when my dad came home, but I would be back. I wished I hadn't said a word about leaving. I still hadn't told him about Breeze.

"What do you mean you aren't going to be in town?"

"Well, I will be in town. But, I met this guy–"

My dad didn't let me finish. He gave me a lecture about how men only want one thing. He didn't let me tell him how Breeze wasn't like any other man. Somehow, my dad brought Eldon back up and talked about how he would be in jail for life if someone ever put their hands on me.

"What does Eldon have to do with Breeze?"

"The point is I haven't met this Breeze, and therefore you are not leaving out of town with him."

"I'm not a teenager. I'm a grown woman living on my own!"

"Beauty, I don't want to hear it."

"Fine, dad. Fine."

"Trust me. It's for your own good. I need you to stay."

"You make it sound like I'm dying or trying to leave and never come back."

"Just listen to your dad for once."

For the first time in my life I had to make a decision to go against my dad. What could he possibly do? Put me on punishment? I chuckled.

"This is no laughing matter," he said.

I let my dad continue the conversation about what his plans were after prison. What he didn't know is that his plans would include Breeze.

After I hung up, I turned the television on. I didn't feel like going to the party, but I really wanted to hang out with Teresa and Kate. I sent a text to see if Teresa was still going with me. She said she didn't want me to pick her up, because she wasn't feeling well. I flipped through the channels with the cable remote and stopped when I saw on screen, a very nice-looking young man with a neatly shaved goatee. His teeth were perfect pearly white and his words thundered like a father chastising a child.

"The time is now. Tough times don't last - tough people do! Give your troubles to God. Let Him take the opportunity to demonstrate His power! Give it to Jesus! People must be introduced to Christ, not to you! Patiently obey God no matter what you may face! Hold on, a change is coming!"

A change is coming? I couldn't answer my own question. His thoughts flowed into expressions of compassion. The man extended his hands directly toward the screen, reaching for my hand and continued to speak.

"Use what you have to live for Jesus, and He will commend you! Leave the door of your heart constantly open to God, and you won't need to worry about hearing his knock. Letting Him in is your only hope for lasting fulfillment. Let Jesus fire up your faith and get you into action!"

The choir in their black and white robes stood behind the young minister as they sung softly. I didn't know the song, but the harmonies made the warmth of God's spirit overflow. I began to cry for many different reasons - Randy, Sarai and Doug's breakup. I tuned back in to the minister's words.

"No one is ever too young to take God seriously and obey Him! The word of God should affect you in a major way, causing many to notice the mighty power of the Lord!"

I was unable to change the channel. After the minister finished his sermon, I went to the bathroom and washed my face. I stared in the mirror and felt as though my life flashed before me. In a matter of seconds I saw me arguing with Randy, the car flipping over, and then blackness. I then saw me staring at my reflection in the mirror. At that very moment, everything was clear. I was going to the Bahamas with Breeze and there was nothing no one could do about it, not even my dad.

I heard my phone chime. It was a text from Kate:

"Beauty! Where r you girl?
R u still coming to the party at the mansion?"

I texted her back:

"On my way."

CHAPTER TWENTY

I arrived at the mansion quicker than expected. There was a beautifully sculpted iron gate with scrolls and swirls. The gate attendant took my name and wrote my license plate number on a piece of yellow paper. A water fountain danced with the lights. It looked like a mini replica of the water show at the Bellagio in Las Vegas. The lights changed from red to blue and then green, dancing in competition for my attention. The mansion was enormous and the bright white paint flowed from the top to the bottom. The brown wooden doors had frosted glass in the center. I could see bodies as they moved in front of the door. I sent Kate a text and told her I was on my way up the stairs to the front door. A few seconds later, she came outside and grabbed me by my hand. We gave each other an endearing hug.

"Oh my gosh Beauty, I'm glad you came," Kate said.

"Me too."

The bellman who stood at the door greeted me and addressed Kate by her last name. There was a staircase on the left and one the right, winding their way to freedom. Kate told me she would give me a tour of the mansion later that night. The chandelier that hung in the center of the foyer sparkled as the crystals waved hi. I couldn't take my eyes off the passage of water that streamed through the house.

"Is that a stream? Inside? Where does it take you?"

"That stream is actually a part of the indoor pool. It flows through a part of the mansion," Kate said.

I couldn't believe it. *Who has a stream that flows to an indoor pool?* Kate introduced me to quite a few people. She told me it was an actual listening party for the upcoming artist Tiffany. Tiffany was beautiful. There was a white gardenia in her long wavy hair.

"Hi Beauty. Kate has told me a lot about you," Tiffany said, reaching for a handshake.

"Hi, I'm Tiffany's manager! I quit my other job! I'm working in the biz full-time!" Kate said.

We all laughed.

"When did this happen Kate? I told you not to leave me at that job!"

Laughing Kate said, "I'll tell you all about it later."

"I'm happy for you Kate. Tiffany, it's nice to meet you."

"I hope you will stick around Beauty, so you can hear my debut single," Tiffany said.

"Definitely."

"All right, I'll be right back. I want to introduce Tiffany to a few more people. Grab a drink and enjoy yourself," Kate said.

"Get a drink, from where?"

Before Kate answered my question, a waiter approached me.

"Dom Pérignon for the lady?" The waiter asked.

"Thank you."

I grabbed a glass from the tray and took a sip from the champagne glass. I followed the stream of water that led to the indoor pool. I passed through a room that had seats chiseled in the wall like a cave. Couples kissed. People laughed. I continued my quest. From afar I could see the indoor pool. Palm trees were planted on one side, and lounge chairs on the other. Quite a few people were sitting at the pool as their legs dangled in the water.

"Beauty Summers—is that you?"

Startled, I turned around. It was Bailey, Althea's brother. My first puppy love.

"Bailey!"

He grabbed me and gave me a hug.

"I've been thinking about you lately," he said.

"You were thinking about me?"

I took a sip of my champagne. It was like a dream come true. I waited all my life for Bailey to think about me, but this time I didn't see the fireworks. My heart continued to beat its normal pattern.

"I was going through Althea's old photos and saw a few pictures we took at the Skate Factory. Remember?"

"Oh yes."

I was embarrassed all over again as I thought about my fall.

Bailey carried my glass as we walked past the pool. An automatic sliding glass door led us to the grounds outside. There was another pool and a Jacuzzi. A few people lounged near the pool and a few were inside the Jacuzzi. We made our way past the tennis courts and walked and talked our way toward the rose gardens. There were big tall bushes neatly trimmed into a maze. We sat on the bench next to the roses. The aroma was pleasant. I thought about the roses that were in the mixed bouquet of flowers Breeze bought me when he picked me up for church.

"This is a beautiful mansion." Bailey handed me back my glass.

"Yeah, not bad. Are you here alone?" He asked.

"No. My friend invited me."

"Oh, so, this friend, why isn't he looking for you now?"

"That's because he is a she and my boyfriend couldn't make it."

Changing the subject, Bailey asked, "Hey did you know this is Seth Barrington's mansion?"

"Really? Seth Barrington?"

Bailey nodded his head in agreement. It all made sense. Seth was the record label owner of SB Records, the number one record company in Los Angeles. Kate dated Seth in between Keaton in Sales and Jackson in Legal. "Well, anyway, what have you been up to lately?" I asked.

He told me about his new business venture of booking artists at venues. That's why he was at the party, to network. We talked for over a couple of hours. Before I knew it, it was almost midnight. Breeze called while Bailey talked about booking Tiffany's next gig. I pulled my phone from my wristlet and gestured to Bailey that I would be right back.

"Hey my Beauty."

"Hi Breeze."

"Are you still at the party with Kate?"

"Yeah."

"I'm finishing up on the set. I'll be on my way home shortly. I'll come get you tomorrow night. We can leave from my house to go to the airport. Are you all packed?"

"Yes I am. I'm really excited to spend a vacation with you."

"You're sweet. That's why I'm never letting you go," Breeze said.

"Same here."

"I'll talk to you later. Text me or call me to let me know you made it home safely."

"Are you trying to see what time I get home?"

"Beauty—trust me. I'm not that kind of guy."

From that moment on, I knew I wanted to spend the rest of my life with Breeze, a man I could trust forever.

"I'll let you know when I make it home."

"All right. Bye," he said.

I walked over to Bailey. We made our way back through the mansion. The DJ announced Tiffany was going to perform one last song. I completely forgot, I was supposed to see her perform. Everyone gathered in front of the stage. I saw Kate standing off to the right. When we made eye contact, she gestured for me to come over.

"Well, it was nice seeing you. Tell Althea I said hi."

I hugged Bailey and kissed him on the cheek. I made my way up the stage and stood next to Kate.

"I've been looking all over for you girl!" Kate yelled in my ear as Tiffany's music drowned most of her words.

"Sorry. I saw an old friend. I know we have a lot to catch up on."

"Yes we do. I'll call you tomorrow. Maybe I can pick you up and you can spend the night like old times."

"I'd love to, but I'm leaving for the Bahamas tomorrow night."

"The Bahamas? Oh we definitely have a lot to catch up on," Kate said.

The crowd went wild as Tiffany performed her song "Don't Throw Away My Love." After Tiffany finished I congratulated her. I'd realized she wasn't wearing the same outfit. She had changed into a short hot pink dress. Her heels made her appear taller than before. She reached into a nearby basket and gave me an autographed CD.

I told Kate I needed to use the restroom before I left.

"Use the bathroom upstairs. There should be less of a crowd. When you come back, I want to give you a tour of the mansion before you leave," Kate said.

I agreed and proceeded to walk toward the winding staircase. I grabbed the rail and gracefully walked up the stairs like I was a movie star. Not paying attention, I tripped up the last step. I played it off and walked toward the middle of the walkway, looking down at the crowd. Everyone seemed happy. Seth stood next to Tiffany and Kate. He held Kate tightly around her waist. The band packed up their stuff as guests made their way out the door. Some people gave the bellman a ticket. He took the ticket and opened the door. Inside the door was a clothing rail like the one at the cleaners. He looked at the ticket and moved the rail with the press of a button.

The crowd became smaller. *I should stop being nosy and use the restroom.* I realized I didn't know which way to go. I decided to go left since I saw a few women come from that direction. I walked down the hall. There were several doors. Some doors were open and some were closed. I peeked through a cracked door and saw a couple kissing and hugging on the bed.

"Go away, unless you want to pay to play," a woman said laughing with a heavy European accent.

I hurriedly closed the door. I saw a waiter walk toward my direction.

"Where is the restroom?"

"You are almost there madam. Walk toward the end of the hall and turn right," he said.

There was a never-ending story to this mansion. On my way I saw two burgundy chaises against the hallway wall and giant bookshelves on opposite sides. The marbled floors were gray and white. I finally arrived at the last door on the right. I pushed open the door and on the floor was a young, thin girl.

"Are you OK?"

"Why does it matter to you? No one cares, especially not daddy. He's going to marry that bitch anyway," she said, holding a razor blade over her wrist.

I had no idea why she was confessing her emotions about her father to me.

"Wait a minute. I know you are not about to kill yourself."

"I can't take it anymore. She told daddy to stop giving me money," she said.

"Who?"

I became concerned. Somehow I identified with the young girl. I knew what is like to feel alone and unwanted. Before I could ask another question, she slit her wrist right before my eyes. The blood instantly drained itself from her body.

"Help, Help!" I yelled.

No one came from my yells of rescue. I dialed 9-1-1 as quickly as I could. The paramedics were on their way. I grabbed an embroidered monogram towel hanging from a rack in the bathroom. I tied the towel around her wrist and held her in my arms. I called Kate. She and Seth immediately came running.

"We took the elevator and came up as quick as we could," Kate said.

"Dear God, I don't need a lawsuit," Seth said.

He gasped as he looked at the girl I was holding.

"Olivia! No, no, no. Not my Livy!" he yelled.

"Who is Livy?" I asked Kate while she tried to console Seth.

"His daughter."

Seth kneeled down and grabbed Olivia from my arms. I felt the coldness of Livy's loneliness, all of my past hurts, Sarai's despair, Teresa's anger, and Randy's death. Teardrop by teardrop my heart weighed a ton; heavier than the last time.

I didn't remember seeing the paramedics when they arrived. I didn't remember getting my car out of valet and I didn't remember sending Breeze a text telling him I made it home safely. All I could remember is feeling emotionally exhausted again. I crawled in my bed, closed my eyes, and said a prayer, asking God to heal us all.

CHAPTER TWENTY-ONE

The ride to the airport from Breeze's seemed like it took forever. The driver didn't say much, although, he was very polite. The airport was like being in another world. People shuffled in and out of cars. Taxicabs blew their horns at pedestrians. Yet again, there was a lot of traffic it was unbelievable. There were lines outside the airport and lines inside the airport. After we stood in the first line to get our tickets, we stood in another to get to the gate. Breeze said ever since 9-11, it took a lot longer to get through the security check. With our flight leaving at night, I thought the airport would be empty.

I was nervous about the whole trip. I had thoughts of "what if?" What if the plane crashed? What if we missed our flight? Just what if? Breeze calmed my nerves whenever I questioned him. He said I had nothing to fear. The security agent motioned for me to walk through the metal detector. The buzzer went off. The agent searched me from head to toe with a handheld metal detector that made noise when it went over the button on my jeans.

"Please spread your arms and legs," the woman said as she patted me down as if I were on my way to jail.

I had never been humiliated in my life.

"Lady, does it really take all of this?"

The agent completely ignored my question.

"Please proceed to pick up your belongings. You may go," she said.

Just like that, the nightmare was over. Breeze stood with all of our belongings waiting for me to put on my sandals, belt, and earrings. I told him that this flying stuff was not off to a great start. He reassured me that when we arrived at the Bahamas everything would change. We had a two-hour wait until the plane left. We decided to grab a bite to eat. After that, we went to the VIP room. Some people sat at the bar, some were asleep in the chairs, while others fiddled with cell phones or computers, and made casual conversation. I walked over to the bar and asked for a drink to calm my nerves and a glass of wine for Breeze. Breeze was busy talking to some guy who noticed him from his talk show. I walked over to Breeze and gave him the glass of wine.

"Let's sit here," Breeze said.

Before I was about to sit comfortably in the plush lounge chair, a young woman in an airline uniform walked up to Breeze and said, "Oh my gosh! You're that talk show host guy! Breeze! Island Breeze. I just love your show!"

"Thank you," Breeze said.

"I would ask you for your autograph, but it's against company's policy to harass entertainers."

"Oh no problem, I'll give it to you."

"No really. I don't want to lose my job. I just wanted to tell you I record your show every night when I'm home. I absolutely love you," she said.

This wasn't my first time experiencing people noticing Breeze, but it made me feel special. I was happy that Breeze wanted to spend his time with me and was thrilled we were on our way to paradise. Time passed by fast. Before I knew it, it was time to get on the plane. When the flight attendant called for First Class, Breeze and I made our way onto the plane. The leather seats didn't look very comfortable, but I was sleepy, it didn't matter. Breeze placed our articles in a bin above our heads, and pulled a pair of headphones from his duffle bag.

"Here, I bought you your first traveling headphones. These will keep you from hearing the sound of the plane when we are in the air. You can use them to listen to the movie they'll show or tune in to the airline radio."

"They're going to show a movie?"

"Yes. Like I told you, it only gets better," he said.

I watched the flight attendant make a speech on how to buckle the seat belt and what to do in case of an emergency. *At least I'm not the only one who lives in the world of "what ifs?"* When the plane took off, I looked out the window and barely saw a thing. I felt like I was headed to the moon. The lights in the city became farther and farther away. I placed the headphones over my ears, tuned to a jazz station, leaned my head back, and closed my eyes. Breeze reached over and grabbed my hand. I looked at him and smiled. He leaned over and kissed me.

"Snacks and beverages will be served shortly," the flight attendant said with an island accent.

I could barely hear the announcement. Breeze was right. The headphones tuned everything out. I was relaxed and drifted off to sleep, finally without any worries.

"Wake up," Breeze said as he gently rubbed my thigh.

"Hunh?"

I'd forgotten I was 30,000 miles up in the sky.

"Slide up the shade."

As I pulled the shade up, my eyes saw the most beautiful blue water. It looked clear, turquoise in fact. I saw small pieces of land as their peaks pierced through the clear waters.

"It's beautiful. I'm glad you cared enough about me to take me on a vacation."

"How could anyone not?" Breeze asked charismatically.

The pilot announced the weather was 85 degrees. He said we would land in the next 30 minutes, and for the flight attendants to prepare for landing. *Prepare for landing?* I didn't ask Breeze what the pilot meant. Almost in tears, I was too fixated on the beauty of God's creation. Looking out the window wasn't as bad as I anticipated. The Bahamas was a perfect paradise. I asked Breeze what our agenda was for the day. He said as soon as we checked in, we could do whatever I wanted. I thought about the pictures I saw of couples riding horses in the water. I remembered reading articles of things to do in the Bahamas, but for one reason or another, I couldn't think of what to tell Breeze what I wanted to do. I began to feel a tingle in my stomach as the plane descended. I gasped for air. Fixated on the plane slowly aligning itself with the runway, I felt tense. Breeze grabbed my hand. The plane landed and the crowd clapped. Slightly dazed, I looked at Breeze.

"Are you OK?" Breeze asked.

Breathing a sigh of relief, I said, "I'm glad to be here with you."

A few minutes later, we unbuckled our seat belts. While the pilot gave a greeting, people stood up and grabbed their belongings. Breeze had to wait for the woman who struggled to pull her bags from the overhead bin. After a few seconds of huffs and puffs, Breeze offered his assistance. The ungrateful woman turned, gave him a half smile, and didn't say thank you when he lowered her luggage.

"You're welcome!" Breeze said.

She didn't say a word as she rolled her bags off the plane. Breeze shook his head in dismay.

"Thank you for flying our airline," the flight attendant said, smiling as she stood next to the pilot.

The pilot gave a slight nod to Breeze as we walked off the plane. After we retrieved our bags, the ride to the hotel did not take long.

"Ahh, we're here, Sandals Resort." Breeze said.

The chauffeur opened my door and helped Breeze with the bags. The beauty of the building and scenery captivated me. The staff was pleasant. This was the best place I'd ever been. After we checked in, we were escorted to a pathway outside. A young man in a golf cart stopped in front of us. He took our bags and gave Breeze and me a brochure of the resort.

"You have a villa on the best side of the resort. It has a beautiful view of the ocean. Every night you'll encounter a beautiful sunset," the man said.

On the way to the villa, two of the hotel workers with drinks on a tray greeted us. The drinks had toothpicks as an umbrella.

"What's the name of this drink?" I asked as she handed both of us a glass.

"This is our special drink for the week. It's called Golden Sunset," the woman said with an accent.

Now that the woman mentioned it, the colors did remind me of a sunset. A few minutes later we arrived at our private beachfront villa. There was another man who greeted us at the door. He took our empty glasses and placed them on his tray.

"Hello ma'am and sir. I'm your butler, Shane, and I'm here to pamper you two to ensure you have a magnificent stay."

"Thank you, Shane," Breeze said.

After Shane and the driver left, I walked around the villa and opened every drawer and closet. The opened French doors led to the private patio. I leaned over the rail. Breeze walked up behind me and gave me a hug. I turned toward Breeze and gave him a passionate kiss. We kissed until we had shortness of breath.

"Thank you for bringing me here."

"You deserve all this and more. Remember, we'll take life one day at a time," we said in unison.

If this was a glimpse of life with Breeze, I didn't want it to end. I continued to explore each room. The villa was fully furnished. The bathroom had a double marble vanity. There were lit candles along the countertop. The glass-enclosed shower had a separate soaking tub. Bubble bath soap sat on the edge of the tub. I loved it. I wanted to pack the soap in my luggage, but I didn't want to seem uncouth. This was too good to be true. The villa was perfect, the moment was perfect, and Breeze was the perfect man for me.

CHAPTER TWENTY-TWO

Awaking from my nap, I heard drums. I walked into the living room and kissed Breeze on his arm while his muscles flexed as he held the phone.

"Well tell Cameron we'll have to shoot an extra episode when I get back. I'm on a vacation. As a matter of fact, I'm turning off my cell phone. Erin, I need you to handle everything. If it's an absolute emergency, just call the front desk. Otherwise, take care of it and I'll be back in a few days."

The conversation ended abruptly with his assistant.

"I want to make sure you have my undivided attention," Breeze said smiling.

"Do you hear those drums?"

"Yeah. I heard this place turns into a party at night."

"Oh yeah? Well, I'm ready to get my groove on," I said, snapping my fingers in the air.

After taking a quick shower and changing clothes, we were ready to follow the sound of the drums. I took a picture of the perfect sunset while the sun waved goodbye. We walked toward the crystal blue water, treading our love on the white sand. There were a few men twirling fire sticks around their head and into their mouth. Their performance was truly magical. We took a small paddleboat to have dinner at a restaurant on the water.

After dinner, we headed for the dance floor. Breeze was a great dancer. I remember Randy and I would hang out at clubs from time to time. I was no stranger to the dance floor. One song led to five and we couldn't dance anymore. We moved to the other side of the restaurant where there were a few pool tables. I had never played pool before, and I couldn't get my aim quite right.

"You can't move the eight ball just so you can hit it!" Breeze exclaimed.

"I can't seem to take this white ball and knock the black ball or any color ball for that matter in those stupid holes!"

Breeze could tell I was frustrated by a simple game of pool.

"Come on, let's head back to the room," he said.

We took the paddleboat back to the main beach. Breeze helped me out of the boat and took my hand. As we walked on the beach, the warm sand between my toes welcomed me. I held my sandals in one hand and wrapped my arm around Breeze's waist with the other.

Seductively I whispered, "This is the most romantic night I've ever had in my life."

"Well, if you stay with me, this won't be the last."

He grabbed my hand and pulled us into the warm tropical water. I threw my shoes on the sand. I reached down to put my hands in the water. I cupped my hands together and threw water on Breeze. He stopped. I froze and then he ran and pushed me down in the water. We both fell. I rolled on top of him and kissed him like there was no tomorrow. I wanted this night to last forever.

The next morning our butler Shane woke us up with a doorbell ring. He wanted to know what we wanted for breakfast. Breeze asked him to bring us French toast and juice. I didn't care what Shane brought us for breakfast.

I was astonished we had a butler. Teresa wouldn't believe me if I told her. After breakfast, we went sailing and then we had the chauffeur take us on a ride through the town. We bought a lot of trinkets, beach towels, clothes, and shoes. I didn't know how I planned to get the extra stuff back home. My luggage was full when I arrived. Next time, I'll know to pack less.

When we arrived back to the resort, Breeze scheduled for us to have a couple's massage. The spa was spectacular. When we finished getting our massage, I turned to Breeze and said, "You know, this is a lifestyle I could definitely get used to." He smiled and pulled me close to his side.

For dinner, Shane prepared steak and lobster. The food was delicious. Breeze and I were full. We fell asleep on the sofa. When we woke up it was after one in the morning. I turned my head and looked out toward the patio. I saw the moon shining against the soft, rippled water. The moment was surreal. I leaned over to Breeze and kissed his soft lips. He kissed me back. He grabbed me and wrapped his legs between mine. I gently moved my hands toward his back. I trembled, full of lust and desire. Pierced with passion sustained from within, that very second, we became one. I pushed out all of my jealousy, hurt, fears, and pain. From that very moment, I breathed a new breath of life, a new life with Breeze.

The next morning we slept in. We stayed at the resort and went horseback riding on the beach. It was one more day of complete perfection. I never knew love could be so serene, full of peace and trust. After horseback riding, we went to one of the nightclubs at the resort. We danced and drank all night long. I don't even know how we made it back to the room. Breeze said he called Shane to come and get us, but honestly, I don't think Breeze remembered how we made it back to the room, either.

Our last day at the resort was bittersweet. We shopped again at a few nearby boutiques. I bought Teresa, Kate, and my dad souvenirs. I couldn't wait to get back to tell Teresa about my trip with Breeze. Breeze suggested we send the stuff we bought via FedEx. He texted Erin to get his FedEx account number. While we packed our bags, Shane came to visit. He shared with us that he had worked for a couple of Sandals resorts. He said our next trip should be to Sandals in Antigua. Breeze said he would definitely put that destination on our to-do list. Despite his resistance, we gave Shane the night off. Breeze handed him his gratuity in an envelope and we bid Shane adieu.

The next morning after check out I took every experience with me and held it close to my heart. Every meal I ate, I savored the flavor. Every activity, every dance, every moment, I wouldn't let it go. Breeze allowed me to experience life, and for this I was grateful.

"Did you enjoy yourself?" Breeze asked as we boarded the plane.

"I can't even begin to tell you what you've done for me."

I was ready to go back home, but the memories we created would last a lifetime. The plane seamlessly lifted into midair. Breeze leaned on the arm of the seat and gave me a heartfelt hug. I fell asleep on the plane, at peace with life again.

Tell me why
I get high
On your chocolate moon
Of lust
Your thrust of
The hips, the
Way you move
Those lips
And sweet tongue
Moisture of lust
Upon each thrust
I pause

DON'T CRY FOR LOVE

On this journey of love
Come here softly
Moving toward a
Century of oneness . . .
Togetherness . . .
I look up
I look around
I close my eyes
And . . .
Just breathe . . .

CHAPTER TWENTY-THREE

When I arrived home the streets were blocked off with police cars and yellow tape. An older Caucasian police officer approached the taxicab driver's window. The cab driver pointed toward me before the officer began to speak. I rolled down the window.

"Hello ma'am. Do you live on this street?" The officer asked.

"Yes. What happened?"

"There was a 419." He cleared his throat and continued, "I mean, a man was found dead inside those apartments. He hung himself."

"Who hung himself?"

I was shocked, nervous, and felt concerned at the same time.

"I don't have all the details, ma'am. May I see some identification to prove you live on this street? We are only allowing the people who live here to pass through. Police are currently investigating the scene."

I reached in my sling bag that Breeze bought me that read the Bahamas—Sandals Resort. I pulled out my driver's license and didn't ask the officer any more questions.

"Oh, you live in the building where the crime took place. One of the officers at the door will escort you to your apartment.

The officer walked to the yellow tape and removed it halfway for the taxicab to pass through. The driver couldn't pull in front of the apartment.

He parked at the "Heights" next door. He popped the trunk and opened my door.

"Would you like me to help you with your bags?" He said holding my luggage.

"No, I'll be fine. Thank you."

I paid and tipped the driver. He thanked me and proceeded to drive back toward the officer who was still holding the tape in his hands. My neighbor Ms. Valley, who lived on the seventh floor, stood outside the apartment with her Teacup Yorkshire Terrier named Sweetie.

"Beauty darling," she said as she rubbed Sweetie's head.

"Hi Ms. Valley."

I met Ms. Valley one day as I was leaving the parking structure. She had many bags of dog food in her hand. I helped her up to her apartment two floors above me. Ms. Valley was a retired flight attendant. Her husband, who was a retired Marine, died a year ago. When Ms. Valley opened her apartment door, I thought it was the Fourth of July. Displayed were more American flags than the White House itself.

"My husband collected American flags," Ms. Valley said.

I guess she noticed how I stared in awe at all the flags. She talked about her profession, but most of her conversation reflected on her husband Thomas, a diehard veteran, who served in the military for 28 years. After my visit, I would see Ms. Valley from time to time, in and out of the parking structure. She invited me to have tea with her a few times. On my second visit, I learned she had one daughter, Abbatha, who lived in Wyoming. Abbatha never returned home after college.

Ms. Valley continued our conversation while the officer stood at the door, waiting for me to come in.

"Oh, you're coming from a vacation, my dear?"

For a moment, I forgot about my perfect vacation with Breeze after contemplating on what had happened.

"Yes, Ms. Valley. I just came back from the Bahamas."

"Oh lovely. I've been there quite a few times."

"Tell me, what happened?" I asked.

"Well, you won't believe it. It's Mr. Bill. He hung himself. The security guard found him when he was making his nightly routine rounds," she said as she raised her hand toward her forehead. "Oh boy. I need a drink," Ms. Valley continued.

"What! Mr. Bill?"

I couldn't believe my ears.

Ms. Valley, you will have to tell me everything tomorrow. I'll come and visit you and we can drink some tea."

"If you want dear, you can come on up now and join me for a drink," she said.

"I think I will pass."

More like pass out. Ms. Valley managed to breathe her pungent breath right into my nostrils. I felt exhausted. Ms. Valley would keep me there for a while, explaining Mr. Bill's death. She threw her hands up in the air. Her gesture didn't change my mind. The officer escorted me to my apartment. On my way to the elevator, the back exit to the parking structure was partitioned with the yellow Do Not Cross tape. Dismayed, I pushed the button to summon the elevator to rescue my thoughts. The door opened. I rolled my luggage and swung my duffle bag over the handle. Exhausted, I unlocked my apartment door.

"Have a good night ma'am. Be sure to lock your door," the officer said.

I smiled at the officer, and closed and locked my door. I didn't unpack. I texted Breeze and told him I made it home. I didn't tell him about Mr. Bill. I was extremely tired and glad to be home. Then I realized . . . my period was definitely late.

CHAPTER TWENTY-FOUR

I slept past noon the next day. I was having the same dream over and over again, and woke up screaming. Sometimes it was different parts of the same dream. I tried frantically to piece the puzzle together, but it was no use. In my dream I received pictures from a man. I couldn't remember who he was. His face was blurry.

In another dream I argued with Randy. I don't know what the argument was about, but I lost control of the car and we crashed. The most recent dream I had was the worst one of all. I dreamt I was in complete darkness. I couldn't see anyone or anything, but heard muffled voices. I felt needles sticking into my hand and in my arm. The room was cold and reeked of death. The air was thick. I couldn't move and could barely breathe.

At one point, the only distinctive voice I heard was Breeze's.

He said, "Just take life one day at a time."

Still I couldn't respond. My stomach was in intense pain. Someone held my hand, but I didn't have enough strength to react. I tried to lift my head or any part of my body. I felt physically and emotionally drained. Too much to bear, I screamed and realized it was just a dream.

I lay in bed and reflected on my collage of dreams. My thoughts drifted away and I subconsciously planned my day. I called Breeze. We talked for over an hour. We shared our favorite moments while we were on vacation. I told him I didn't have any bad dreams while I was in the Bahamas, but I had them again last night. He told me to release my thoughts because something was troubling me. He rambled something about me having lucid dreams. He went on to say that I should do some research on my dreams to find out what bothered me.

"Well, let me know what you find on the Internet about lucid dreams. I have to get back to work. I should be finished in a couple of hours. Would you like to hang out at Joi's?" He asked.

I agreed. We said our goodbyes and anticipated spending time together again at Joi's.

I decided to surprise Teresa. She was thrilled I stopped by. When I arrived at her door, Stack was inside. *What was Stack doing in Teresa's apartment?*

"It's time you know about Stack and me," Teresa said.

I opened my mouth in awe, but no words followed my jester. I looked over at Stack as he arranged the playing cards in his hand.

"What?" He said nonchalantly.

I turned my head toward Teresa for an explanation.

"I started seeing Stack several months ago. I just didn't know how to tell you."

"Teresa, I knew I heard his voice one day when I came over. You said it probably was the TV!"

I pushed Teresa's arm. She laughed. I was not amused. Stack, of all people, was just like Randy. A womanizer, not to mention, he did have a baby with Farah, who used to hang out with us. I shook my head in disbelief. I released my personal feelings of disgust for Stack and joined in the next card game.

"Stack, how many kids do you have now?" I couldn't resist the question.

"Beauty, please, don't start," Teresa said.

"Don't start?" I repeated. "I can't believe you Teresa! Stack of all people?"

I momentarily forgot Stack was sitting right next to us.

"What is that supposed to mean? I thought we were cool?" Stack asked.

"Stack, let's face it. No offense, but I think Teresa can do better."

"Really Beauty? Better than Randy, I suppose?" She blurted.

I couldn't believe Teresa said those hateful words.

"Never mind Teresa, I'll talk to you later."

I grabbed my purse and keys and stormed out of her apartment.

When I arrived home, I immediately grabbed my cell phone I'd accidentally left on the sofa. I had a few missed messages from my dad and Teresa. I didn't want to talk to Teresa so I called my dad.

"Hey baby girl. I've been trying to reach you."

"Hey dad. I forgot my cell phone at home today."

"Where are you?" He asked.

"I'm home."

"Great! I'm on my way."

"What do you mean you're on your way?

"Exactly what it sounds like. I . . . will . . . be . . . there . . . in a few . . . minutes . . . " He said repeating each word slowly.

"OK dad. I can't wait to see you."

I was excited. I hadn't seen my dad for over a year and a half. He hung up and ended the conversation without saying goodbye as usual. Sometimes that really annoyed me, but today I didn't mind. I had to decide how to break the news to my dad about Breeze. I sat down on the sofa and picked up a magazine I had on the table. Before I knew it I read the entire magazine.

There was a knock at the door. I walked to my door and wondered how my dad made it into the building without buzzing the intercom. I looked through the peephole. It was Ms. Valley wearing her American flag sun visor, holding Sweetie.

I opened the door and asked Ms. Valley to have a seat on the sofa. I guess she wasn't sure if I was still coming over for tea, since it was nearing the evening.

"Hi Ms. Valley."

"I know you said you were coming to my apartment for tea, but instead I wanted to visit you. Not to mention, I completely forgot to ask you how you were doing last night. You know, with the loss of Randy and all," she leaned toward me and said.

This time I held my breath.

"Oh, that's very thoughtful of you. I'm managing, I suppose."

Ms. Valley made her way to the sofa, and held on to the arm of the sofa as she slowly sat down. I reached out my arms and grabbed Sweetie.

"Oh," Ms. Valley said as she handed Sweetie to me. "I don't move as fast as I used to."

"It's OK Ms. Valley, take your time."

Ms. Valley reminded me of the grandmother I never had. Each crease on her face indicated years of wisdom. Her gray hair was brushed into a ponytail, while several strands haphazardly lay along the side of her face. She moved one curl away from her eye with the back of her wrinkled hands. Ms. Valley kept me company for over an hour. She told me how she emotionally dealt with the death of her husband.

"What 'cha writing there?" She asked as she pointed to an opened tablet on the table.

"Oh, just a few poems."

"Well, why don't you read this old lady a poem or two?"

I couldn't say no to Ms. Valley. Her pleasant smile impelled me to lean forward and pick up the tablet. I flipped a couple of pages and rolled them behind. Ms. Valley leaned forward, her curiosity increasing.

DON'T CRY FOR LOVE

"This poem, Ms. Valley, is called 'Heartbeat.' "

"Heartbeat," she repeated as she leaned back on the sofa, holding Sweetie close to her heart.

Bump—Bump
I gently feel his heartbeat
I lay my head on his chest
I whisper to his soul

Bump—Bump
Don't stop, don't move
'Cause I'm loving the vibe
This is one drug
That has me on a natural high
Bump—Bump

Can't pull away from this
God-given sound
As he gently flexes
His soul begins to speak

Bump—Bump
Oohh, I'm too far deep
Won't someone please
Wake me from this nocturnal sleep?

These recurring dreams
What's the deal?
I can't tell the difference
From the fake or the real

Bump—Bump
Shhh, now go on and rest
For this is how I must relieve
My days full of stress

His heartbeat
You have to believe
I reminisce
To be deceived
Love don't live here any more
I wanna say . . . Ummm

Bump—Bump
I listen,
Bump—Bump
The earth stops
Bump—
My soul moves
Bump—
I awake
And my life still continues . . .

After I read the last word, I looked over to Ms. Valley as she reached to wipe her eyes.

"Ms. Valley, are you OK?"

"That was absolutely brilliant, darling. You need to have your work published. Kick that old habit of fear and stand on the stage, if it is the last thing you do."

I didn't tell Ms. Valley I had stage fright, nor did I bother to ask her how she knew. Ms. Valley wobbled to gain her posture. I picked Sweetie up and helped Ms. Valley off the sofa.

"These old legs aren't as strong they used to be. Remember my dear, you can do anything you want to. When you get on stage, just close your eyes and let your soul guide your fear away," Ms. Valley said as she walked toward the door. "Let me know how it goes," she continued to say with a reassuring smile.

Sweetie barked as if he agreed with Ms. Valley.

"Let you know how what goes?"

"Your stage performance," she said as she opened the door.

Ms. Valley reached over and gave me a hug and whispered in my ear, "You can do it; you can do it."

This time, I didn't focus on the bitter smell of her breath, but rather the sweet-smelling words of encouragement. Ms. Valley was right. I was ready to conquer my fear.

After Ms. Valley left, my dad arrived. He and I were thrilled to see one another. We talked about what life was like when he was a kid all the way to Breeze. He embraced my feelings for Breeze after all.

"As long as my daughter is happy, but . . . "

I didn't let him finish. I cut his thoughts off and asked if he remembered the time when we went bike riding. It was late one Saturday evening. Shortly after Charity died, my dad drank heavily. I'd noticed he was intoxicated because he slurred his words. I told my dad I wasn't in the mood to go bike riding, let alone with him. He used his authoritative voice and instructed me to get his bike out the garage. He had a black beach cruiser. I walked in the deep, dark, cold garage and turned on the florescent light. I could barely see. I hated going inside the garage. The construction was not complete. You could see the wood beams, as strips of wood flaked on certain parts. *Ouch!* I kicked my knee on the lawnmower my dad never used.

Interestingly, my dad did not recall the story the way I told it. He said I asked him could we go bike riding.

"Dad, why would I ask you to do that at night?"

He didn't respond.

I made my way over to the corner of the garage and ran into a spider web. *Yuk!* I wiped my face. I hoped the spider fell to the ground and not in my hair. The bike and I fought while I dragged it out the garage. I won and brought it to the front of the house.

Exasperated, I shouted to my dad, "The bike is out!"

He stumbled his way toward my direction. His uncoordinated movements agitated me.

"Get on," he said.

I stood on my tippy toes and held onto the handlebars.

"Sit on the seat!" He yelled.

My dad crossed over the bike and pushed his weight on the pedal.

I complained, "I want to go back home."

"No. I recalled you said 'this is fun daddy!' " He said interrupting my story.

Even though our stories didn't fully agree, we concurred on one thing: after a few times around the block, his lack of soberness caused us to fall to the ground.

"OK, I do remember that," my dad said laughing.

"I still have a scar on my knee, dad!"

He didn't apologize then and he didn't apologize now. That was my dad. He never admitted when he was wrong, and he never said he was sorry.

CHAPTER TWENTY-FIVE

Don't be afraid
Death whispers in my ear
I sometimes feel
Death is really near.

I try to escape
When death calls my name
It desperately wants to pull me
Into its great hall of fame

I can't stop hearing
Death's call on my mind
Please Lord, not now
I'm lost, but still trying to find

Find my way
Down roads here and there
Not sure where to go
As death continues to stare

Death, oh death
Just let me be
Until I'm ready
For you to consume me

Breeze called to see if I wanted to have lunch at the pier. I was a bit tired, but I said yes. After writing the poem about death I became depressed. I constantly thought about Randy. I reflected on his infidelity. I thought about Teresa. She dropped the bomb last week that Stack got her pregnant. I cried at her hateful words, even though she apologized. I cried when I thought about Sarai and the loss of her love. I felt compassion for Livy, the girl who slit her wrist.

Suddenly, the walls closed in. I passed the state of depression to the point of no return. I needed Breeze more than ever. His touch alone made me feel like I had no worry in the world. His infectious smile turned my days into tranquil nights. I was glad we met. One problem remained: I could not piece my dreams together.

I changed my thoughts into a positive direction and thought about the conversation I had with Ms. Valley a week ago. She was right. I could conquer my fear of stage fright. That moment I had an epiphany. I decided to call everyone I knew and told them to meet me at Joi's tomorrow night. I was going to do the unthinkable. I was going to get on stage and conquer my fear. Everyone I spoke to was supportive and ensured me they wouldn't miss my performance.

I went up to Ms. Valley's apartment to share the good news. I knocked on the door three times. She didn't answer. Sweetie faintly barked behind the locked door. I went back to my apartment and wrote a note to Ms. Valley:

Dear Ms. Valley,

Thank you for giving me the words of encouragement. I'm going to take your advice and recite my poem on stage tomorrow at Joi's. I wish you could be there, but I'll be sure to tell you all about it over a cup of tea.

Sincerely,
Beauty Summers

I folded the paper and put it in an envelope. I went back to Ms. Valley's apartment and slid the envelope under the door, hoping Sweetie didn't think it was her next meal.

Breeze picked me up shortly thereafter. I told him how I was nervous about getting on stage at Joi's. He reassured me that I would be just fine.

"Did you call Joi and tell her the great news?" Breeze asked.

"Oh no! I completely forgot. I told everyone to meet me at Joi's tomorrow. I should've called Joi first."

"Everything will be all right. Why don't you call her now?"

It was a little after noon. I wasn't quite sure if Joi or anyone would be there to answer the phone. I called Joi's. There was no answer, so I left a message on the answering machine. Upset at my own defeat, I feel asleep in the car on the way to the pier.

Suddenly, I sat up and looked out the window. A car was toppled upside down. Firefighters rushed to pull the victims from the car. Somehow, I managed to capture a glimpse of the driver as she yelled for help, banging on the window. The look of terror in her eyes—and the fear in mine. I realized I was the driver—a reflection of myself. I couldn't believe what happened. I turned to Breeze. He was not there. No comfort or support from the man who taught me how to love life. I glanced back at the trapped image of me. Our eyes locked.

"Beauty! Help me! Help me!" My reflection yelled.

My mouth coordinated with hers. I turned away in hopes the terror would end. I closed my eyes and held my breath. The pain in my stomach was back. I was breathing rapidly. The warm tears fell against my cheeks. Darkness engulfed my vision. I heard the same muffled voices. They were unnoticeable. I tried to silence my pain, thoughts, and fears.

"Wake up sleeping Beauty. We're here," Breeze said.

I felt Breeze's hand on my arm. I opened my eyes in awe of reality. I looked around. The sun's rays fell fresh on my skin. The beach water looked more beautiful than ever. The calm waters caused my anxiety to subside. Slowly, I looked to my right. There was no sign of a firefighter, a car turned upside down, or the woman who looked like me.

"Were you having one of your dreams again?" He asked.

I had to get out of the car. When I opened the door, I was in such a rush. I lost my balance and fell to the ground. I hit my head on the adjacent parked car.

"Ouch!"

"Beauty!" Breeze yelled.

He rushed to my side. He knelt down and helped me up. He picked up my embarrassment off the ground and threw it in the ocean. He held me tight. I couldn't stop crying.

Breeze looked me in my eyes and said, "It's going to be all right. I'm here for you. Just take life one day at a time. You'll see. Life will deal you a hand, but you have to know how to play it. Sometimes we make the wrong play and sometimes we make the right play. Just hold on to those plays that are right."

I nodded my head in agreement. He picked up my purse off the ground and closed the door. I brushed off the dirt on my jeans. When we walked along the wooded pier, my phone rang. I didn't recognize the number. I almost didn't answer it, until Breeze reminded me it could be Joi, and it was. We talked for a few minutes. I looked at Breeze for support.

He whispered, "You can do this."

On our way to the restaurant we stopped by a few vendors to look at jewelry and T-shirts. We laughed at one that read, I'M WITH STUPID.

"I've seen these before, but I'd never wear it," Breeze said.

"I would."

"Oh yeah?"

He pushed my arm. We started to play fight. I chased him to the restaurant. We were like two teenagers who were madly in love. I jumped on his back as he carried me up the stairs. People stared and I didn't care. I was with Breeze.

CHAPTER TWENTY-SIX

My heart pounded. Perspiration soaked my shirt as I imagined myself on stage at Joi's. *I know I can conquer this fear.* I paced back and forth on the phone with Breeze, contemplating if I could recite my poem tonight.

"My sweet Beauty," Breeze said.

I held the phone tight.

"Breeze, I don't think I can do this."

"Whoa! Where is that coming from? I'll be there. Your dad and Teresa will be there. We will all be there."

"I know, but what if I forget my poem? What if . . . ."

Breeze didn't let me begin to talk myself out of it.

"You've come this far. Why stop now? Remember, you can do this."

I sighed. "OK."

There was an incoming call. It was Kate. I told Breeze I would call him back later.

"Guess who I ran into last night at Club Red?" Kate said excitedly.

"Who?"

"Sarai!"

"Sarai? Who used to live next door to me?"

"Yeah. We were sitting at the bar and she started a conversation. Long story short, I found out she was your friend Sarai. Small world, right?"

"That's unbelievable! Are you sure that's the Sarai who used to live next door to me? You know she moved to Chicago."

"I know. She's back. She said she was glad we met, because after she moved to Chicago, she lost all her contacts in her phone. We talked about your gift of writing poetry."

That explained why I never heard from Sarai.

"Kate, I'm having second thoughts about tonight."

"Well, you have to perform. I told Sarai about your debut and she said she would be there. Act surprised when you see her, because she wants it to be a surprise."

We laughed, because we both knew Kate could not keep secrets.

"Remember Beauty, you can do it."

"Everyone keeps telling me that, but it's not working."

"Just think of it as a once in a lifetime opportunity. If you never live to see tomorrow, wouldn't you want to make your dream come true? You've always told me you wanted to be on stage at Joi's."

I realized I had to recite my poem, not for everyone else, but for myself.

"You're right. I can and will do this."

"Good. You know Seth and I will be there to support you!"

Kate told me she heard an announcement on the radio.

"They mentioned Floetic Mystress; isn't that your stage name?"

"Yes."

I nearly fainted. I didn't understand how there was an announcement on the radio. I just told Joi yesterday I was going to perform tonight.

"I'm glad you are finally doing this Beauty. Can you believe it?"

"I know. It's like this is all a dream."

"Well, in that case, give it all you've got."

"Yes. Yes. I can and will."

"That's my girl. I'll see you tonight. Are there seats reserved? Valet parking?" Kate asked.

"Yes. There are a few tables Joi reserved for me. There is a large parking lot next to the café, but no valet parking."

We laughed and finished the conversation. I told Kate I would see her and Seth tonight.

I thought about which poem I was going to recite at Joi's. I sat down on the sofa and reached for my tablet of poems. I pulled out every poem I'd ever written. I read them one by one; page by page; prose by prose. Crying, I felt liberated from my fear of stage fright.

CHAPTER TWENTY-SEVEN

There was a knock at the door.

I asked who it was, but there was no answer. The person knocked again. I moved slowly toward the door and looked though the peephole. It was a man who had performed on stage at Joi's.

"Can I help you?"

"You don't know me Beauty, but I really need to talk to you. I have something you need to see."

I didn't open the door. *How did he know my name?*

"I bet you're wondering how I know your name. My name is Titus. I know your little boyfriend . . . Randy. Don't worry, just look in the envelope."

He slid with force a manila folder under the door. My heart pounded hard to the point it ached. *How did Titus know Randy?* I leaned over the envelope with fear. I picked up the light envelope and considered opening the door. Titus was silent. I looked through the peephole again. He was gone. I sat on the arm of the sofa and opened the envelope. Inside was a smaller envelope that read, "YOU SHOULD KNOW." I pulled a few pictures that were turned over, horrified by the images.

There were pictures of Randy with Titus. It was a picture of them sitting on a sofa kissing and a picture with Randy holding his hand toward the camera, as if he was trying to cover his face. Another picture showed them hugging, and a third showed Randy kissing a girl who was pregnant. I took the pictures and flung them on the floor.

"No. No. This can't be!" I screamed and cried hysterically.

I regained my composure and grabbed the pictures and car keys. I was at the point of no return. I tried to call Randy but as usual, he didn't answer. I decided to go to his job.

"Hey, what are you doing here?" Randy asked.

I didn't say a word. I threw the pictures toward his face. He looked at the pictures as they fell haphazardly to the ground.

"Wait. I can explain," he said as he scampered to pick up the pictures off the ground.

"How can you possibly explain this?"

"Let's go outside to the car. Please don't make a scene here," he said.

"I'm never getting in the car with you! I want you out of my apartment and out of my life. I don't know who you are anymore!"

"Please. Let me explain."

For some reason, I gave him the benefit of the doubt. We walked briskly to my car while he tried to rationalize what I saw in those horrible pictures. I started the car and shifted to reverse.

"Wait! I can't leave my job," Randy said.

I ignored his plea. I drove as we yelled back and forth. I couldn't believe my ears. Randy said he met Titus at a party. He talked about how one thing led to another and they developed a relationship. He said he wasn't a homosexual. He just enjoyed the attention Titus gave him. He then went on to say he started dating Titus' sister Amber, and got her pregnant by mistake. The more I heard, the more I became enraged.

"How could you treat me like this?"

I reached over and slapped Randy in the face. Randy held the side of his cheek.

"I know you're upset, but you need to slow this car down."

I took my eyes of the road and yelled, "I hate you!"

"Look out!" Randy yelled.

I turned my head back to the road. I lost control of the car and hit the divider. The car went airborne. We landed upside down. I noticed Randy wasn't breathing.

"Randy! Randy!"

I tried to unbuckle my seat belt as the black smoke appeared. In a panic, I banged on the window.

"Help me, help me!"

No one replied. My world was cold and dim. Everything went black. Randy was pronounced dead at the scene. I was rushed to the hospital as the paramedics tried to save my life.

CHAPTER TWENTY-EIGHT

The nurse walked in the hospital room, humming as she checked Beauty's IV.

"How are you feeling today, Beauty?" Nurse Angelica said, even though she knew Beauty could not respond.

"Your favorite show is coming on in a half an hour. I'll be back to make sure it's on for you."

Nurse Angelica walked out the door, glanced back at Beauty, and smiled.

"Has the doctor checked on the patient in 1127B?" Angelica asked the head nurse.

Nurse Tanner shook her head no, taking a sip from a bottle of water.

"Dr. Kipling will be in shortly. He asked the family to meet him here. He needs to keep them abreast of the patient's situation," Nurse Tanner said.

"Well, I hope he comes after her favorite show is over. I'd hate for Beauty to miss it on account of Dr. Kipling," Nurse Angelica said.

They both laughed as they went in two separate directions, making their way to other patients.

"Teresa, hey it's me," Mr. Summers said.

"Hi. How's Beauty?"

Mr. Summers paused.

"She's not doing too well. The doctor asked for us to come to the hospital as soon as possible."

"OK. I'll be there shortly. I'll call Kate and Sarai. Is there anybody else you'd like me to contact?"

"No Teresa. You've done enough. Thank you," Beauty's dad said.

He hung up the phone, holding back his tears. He thought about Charity when she died. He didn't cry, but he still missed her. He grabbed his coat and left for the hospital.

The ride to the hospital seemed like a lifetime. Traffic on the 405 was a nightmare.

"Why is there always traffic on this damn 405!" Mr. Summers shouted.

His world was turned upside down. No amount of money could make things go back to the way they were. Frustrated, Mr. Summers drove his truck in the shoulder lane. People honked and he honked back. Time was of the essence. He had to get to the hospital soon.

"Beauty, it's that time," Nurse Angelica said.

"Thank you for tuning in to *Island Breeze*, with the one and only Breeze. Where I always say, take life one day at a time," the talk show host said.

"Beauty, I can see why your friend said you were crazy about this show. She said you never missed an episode. Breeze sure is handsome," Nurse Angelica said.

Teresa walked in as the nurse adjusted the television volume.

"Do you turn this on for her every day?" Teresa asked.

"I sure do, and the night nurse turns it on at night for the new episodes. Even though Beauty is in a coma, she may very well hear everything."

Teresa smiled. She remembered how Beauty talked about Breeze as if she really knew him. She joked many times how she would leave Randy for Breeze. Teresa's eyes filled with tears. The nurse gently brushed the side of Teresa's arm as Teresa laid her hand on Beauty's growing belly.

Teresa spoke softly and grabbed Beauty's hand, "Beauty, you have to wake up from this coma. Four months is long enough, OK? You have a baby inside of you that wants to see you. We all want to see you. I miss you."

Teresa's tears fell on Beauty's arm. Teresa grabbed a chair and sat next to Beauty's bed. She watched *Island Breeze* while she teased Beauty about Breeze, just like old times.

"Beauty. Can you hear me? I'm here. Your dad is on his way. I think Kate and Sarai are coming too. Please Beauty. Squeeze my hand. Move your eyes. Just do something to let me know you can hear me," Teresa pleaded.

Beauty didn't move. The roar of laughter from the audience on the television filled the stale air. Teresa could not hold it any longer and gave a loud scream. The nurses came in and immediately consoled her.

About an hour later, Mr. Summers walked in. Teresa had fallen asleep in the chair, still seated next to Beauty. He softly touched Teresa on the shoulder. Startled, Teresa rubbed her stomach to calm her moving baby inside her womb. Mr. Summers knelt down and gave Teresa a tender hug.

"I didn't mean to frighten you. How's she doing?" he asked.

She looked back over at Beauty, and wept.

"Hey, you have to take it easy. You can't have any stress," Mr. Summers said.

"Yeah. I know. I'm OK." Teresa said sniffling and wiping her eyes.

"How's Beauty's baby? Has the nurse updated you on anything?"

"No, the nurse hasn't said anything. She mentioned that Dr. Kipling was waiting for you to arrive."

A few minutes later, Kate and Sarai walked through the door. Each rushed to opposite sides of Beauty's bed.

"Hi Mr. Summers. Hey Beauty. It's Kate. I have a lot to tell you."

Sarai was at lost for words. Tears fell as she rubbed the side of Beauty's face.

Mr. Summers broke the silence.

"Listen, I'm glad you all are here. This means a lot to me. I'll let the nurse know she can get Dr. Kipling to come in and talk to us."

Mr. Summers wanted to cry, but he knew he had to be strong for everyone else. He walked toward the nurse's station, but detoured to the restroom. He walked inside the restroom and let his feelings fall to the floor. He cried like he had never cried before as he knelt on the floor. He didn't care who walked in the restroom and saw him hurting for his one and only daughter. He couldn't do anything to make Beauty come out of a coma.

Minutes later, he finally gained the strength to stand up straight. He grabbed some tissue and blew his nose. He went toward the sink and splashed cold water on his face. He looked at his face in the mirror as the water dripped from his chin into the sink. He grabbed some paper towels and wiped his face. The pain was too much to bear. He couldn't imagine life without Beauty. He took a deep breath and gained his composure. He left the restroom and dreadfully made his way toward the nurse's station.

"I'm ready to speak with Dr. Kipling," Mr. Summers said.

CHAPTER TWENTY-NINE

No seats were available at Joi's. Some people stood along the walls while others waited outside. Every poet was in sight: Cyfin, Black Thunder, Mama Jones, Sizzle, and a few others. Rumors traveled that I would perform tonight. The line outside continued to grow, even though there was no room inside. Sarai was there, just as Kate had said. It was hard for me to act surprised. I looked around and saw all of my friends. I remembered the night I met Breeze at Joi's; the night Sarai and I kicked each other under the table. I smiled as I reflected on how close I had become with my friends since Randy's death.

Joi walked on stage, pointing and waving at people in the crowd. She stood in front of the microphone, excited about tonight's performance.

"Tonight I am thrilled to introduce someone I have asked, time and time again, to get on this stage, and tonight's the night! It's like tonight is a dream come true. Please, everyone put your hands together for Floetic Mystress."

Breeze stood up and pulled my chair away from the table. I looked across the room. I saw my dad who stood at the back of the café, wearing a brim hat. I motioned for my dad to come over. He didn't budge. Instead, he gave me a thumbs-up; like he always did when he was proud of me. I raised my thumb back in approval. My dad's smile was priceless. From that moment on, I knew she could get on stage and recite my poem. I reached for the glass on the table and took a quick sip. I reached over and kissed Breeze.

The crowd cheered as I walked up the side steps onto the stage. I saw Cyfin seated on the side. Cyfin smiled and gave me a nod of approval as she yelled, "Be at peace!"

I stood on stage and felt completely happy about everything. The spotlight shined as bright like the sun on a hot summer day. All my fear subsided as sweat fell from the side of my face.

"You can do it!" Sarai yelled.

I placed my clammy hands on the microphone stand and took the microphone off the hook. Soft music played in the background, I closed my eyes and became one with darkness.

CHAPTER THIRTY

"Mr. Summers, your daughter's condition is getting worse," Dr. Kipling said.

"What do you mean, Doc?"

"Her heartbeat has slowed. We need to deliver the baby, if you want the baby to live."

"And if I decide not to, then what?"

"Then we will lose the baby and possibly lose Beauty, too. She has a 25% chance of survival after we deliver the baby."

Dr. Kipling touched Mr. Summers' shoulder and gave him a firm grip.

"Please let me know your decision. We have to operate immediately, if you decide to save the baby. I'll be back in momentarily."

Mr. Summers became weak. He sat slumped in the chair, which was seated next to Beauty. Teresa walked over to Mr. Summers and rubbed his back for comfort. Both Sarai and Kate cried. Mr. Summers couldn't believe the decision he had to make — save his grandchild in hopes of saving his daughter, or lose them both. The theme song from *Island Breeze* sounded from the television. Natalie, Ms. Henderson, and Aunt Elizabeth walked in. They were surprised to find everyone there. A few times they came, no one was in the room with Beauty. The nurse would always inform them that Beauty was fine and she would hopefully pull through soon.

"What's going on?" Aunt Elizabeth asked.

"The doctor said Beauty is not doing well," Teresa said.

No one else said anything.

"Could everyone please give me a minute to think this thing through?" Mr. Summers asked.

Perplexed, Aunt Elizabeth, Ms. Henderson, and Natalie walked out the room. Teresa, Sarai, and Kate followed. Teresa informed Natalie, Ms. Henderson, and Aunt Elizabeth on Beauty's health condition. Mr. Summers heard Aunt Elizabeth yell, which made the situation completely unbearable. Helplessly, Mr. Summers leaned over Beauty and cried. He remembered the day Beauty's mother told him she was pregnant.

"Chuck, I don't know how you will take this. I know we haven't been together for a long time, but . . . "

"But what, Beverly?" Mr. Summers asked.

"I'm six weeks pregnant."

He didn't react. Mr. Summers continued to count the money in his briefcase.

After he placed the money slowly in a stack he said, "I'm just kidding! That's great! I'm happy! Man! I'm going to be a father!"

He hugged Beverly and twirled her around.

Mr. Summers rubbed Beauty's face with adornment.

"Beauty, for once daddy doesn't know what to do, but I know I need to do this for you."

With a heavy heart, Mr. Summers walked over to everyone who stood outside the hospital room.

"Why don't each of you go in and talk to Beauty one at time, while I get some fresh air," Mr. Summers said.

Natalie went first. She walked in and closed the door. Teresa was on edge, because she didn't trust Natalie. Natalie walked toward the bed with animosity. She grabbed the arms of the bed and leaned in close. She whispered in Beauty's ear, "I know you killed my brother. I know you did it on purpose. I hope you die, and go to hell."

Saliva flew from her mouth as the hateful words pierced the atmosphere, like the stab of a knife killing its victim.

Teresa couldn't take it any longer. She flung the door open.

"What the hell are you doing, Natalie?"

"I was just bidding poor Beauty farewell."

Natalie gawked at Teresa. She brushed past her with a sinister laugh. Without responding, Teresa sat back in the chair next to Beauty. She didn't know what to say or do.

"My hormones are all over the place, Beauty. I can only imagine what you are feeling. You know, your dad has to decide if he will save you or the baby. If you could speak, I know you would want us to save the baby."

She rubbed Beauty's perfect protruding belly.

"Beauty, you're my best friend. We were supposed to shop for baby clothes together. Beauty, please wake up. Please! Please!" Teresa exclaimed.

Sarai heard Teresa crying. She rushed in and pulled Teresa out the chair.

"Teresa, you have to take it easy before you have your baby!" Sarai said.

Teresa couldn't stop crying. Sarai walked Teresa out the room in hopes she would calm down. Ms. Henderson and Aunt Elizabeth walked in. Aunt Elizabeth immediately prayed for Beauty. "Lord, if it's in your will please bring Beauty out of this coma and let her baby be born healthy. We know you know what's best. We ask you in Jesus' name. Amen."

Aunt Elizabeth kissed Beauty on the forehead.

"Be at peace, my dear child. Be at peace," Aunt Elizabeth said as she placed her purple handkerchief over her mouth.

Ms. Henderson leaned over and kissed Beauty on the cheek. Beauty was like a daughter. She lost Randy, and wasn't too sure if Beauty would live. She chuckled. Aunt Elizabeth looked at her sister in dismay.

"You know, I remember when Randy brought Beauty over for the first time. She didn't say much, but I could tell she loved my Randy," Ms. Henderson said as she pushed Beauty's bangs away from her eyes.

Ms. Henderson walked towards her sister. They both touched Beauty's arm one last time. The ventilator beeped as Beauty laid lifeless, but as beautiful as ever. Aunt Elizabeth reached over the feeding tubes and felt Beauty's belly.

"She'll be all right," Aunt Elizabeth said.

Both women stood there in hopes Beauty would move or open her eyes. When both sisters walked out, Kate and Sarai walked in.

"I can't stand hospitals or hospital smells for that matter," Sarai said.

"Yeah. I'm totally not a fan of them, either."

Kate turned to Beauty and said, "Hey Beauty, it's your girls, Kate and Sarai. I don't know where to begin or end, so I won't do either. We had a lot of fun together at work — our Taco Tuesdays, Margarita Fridays, our road trips . . . ."

Reality settled in as Kate spoke to Beauty. Sarai tried to console her, but it was useless.

"Too bad your boyfriend Breeze isn't here. She'd get up for him," Sarai said.

"Beauty never mentioned him. Who's Breeze?" Kate asked sniffling.

"Who is Breeze?" Sarai laughed and continued to say, "Girl, everyone knows he's Beauty's celebrity boyfriend. She always talked about him. While we were waiting outside, Teresa said Beauty told her Breeze asked her out on a date. She embellished the story and said they went to his church and the zoo. The zoo of all places!"

"Beauty has such a sense of humor," Kate said.

"And she's probably dreaming of Breeze right now. I remember she told me that she wish he would whisk her away on a vacation to the Bahamas. Every time she said that, I laughed, because everyone knows Beauty hates to fly."

Both Sarai and Kate laughed.

Mr. Summers interrupted their conversation. "Can I talk to you two out here?"

Kate and Sarai froze. Mr. Summers stood in the doorway and motioned for the two women to follow him.

"Here I am, in the middle of the road. Do I try to save my grandbaby or hope Beauty recovers from a coma? The doctor said it will be a preterm birth, and the baby will have to stay in the hospital until the baby is healthy enough to come home."

"How far along is Beauty?" Kate inquired.

"The doctor said she's 26 weeks."

"About a month before the accident, Beauty told me she was almost two months late for her period. I scolded her and told her to go to the doctor. I should've taken her myself," Teresa said.

"Now is not the time to blame yourself for anything. I have a bigger problem," Mr. Summers said. "As you all know, Beauty has been in a coma for several months. The pregnancy is causing stress to my daughter's body each day."

Dr. Kipling walked toward Mr. Summers as he spoke among friends.

Mr. Summers looked at the doctor like a cat trapped with fear in a tree, "Dr. Kipling, please try and save my daughter and grandbaby."

"We support you no matter what Mr. Summers," Teresa said grabbing Mr. Summers' hand.

Dr. Kipling instructed the nurses to prep Beauty for surgery and asked everyone to wait in the family waiting room. Natalie instantly made up an excuse that she did not feel well and would take a cab home. Mr. Summers could not sit. He paced back and forth, inside and outside the waiting room. Ms. Henderson watched TV and Aunt Elizabeth read her Bible. Kate and Sarai continued to share stories about Beauty. Teresa fell asleep, hoping to awaken from this nightmare.

An hour and a half later, the doctor arrived at the waiting room. "Mr. Summers," Dr. Kipling said in his scrubs.

Mr. Summers held his breath. Everyone's attention was on Dr. Kipling. Teresa opened her eyes and rubbed her stomach. Mr. Summers walked closer to Dr. Kipling, hanging on to every word.

"I have some good news and some bad news," the doctor said.

"Just give it to me straight Doc," Mr. Summers said.

"It's a boy," the doctor said raising both hands in the air.

Everyone cheered and couldn't wait to see the baby. Mr. Summers sighed with relief.

"You all can see the baby in about an hour on the third floor. Under the circumstances, I've asked the nurse to allow everyone in the nursery. You won't be able to hold the baby, because he is very small. We'll place him in an incubator, and we'll put him close to the viewing window for all to see."

"What's the bad news?" Teresa blurted.

"Well, the bad news is . . . "

The doctor looked at Beauty's dad with deep regret. Mr. Summers felt a sharp pain in his heart.

"It's Beauty. She didn't make it. I'm sorry," the doctor said.

In an instant, everyone forgot the good news. Their hearts grieved with pain.

"We'll let you say goodbye Mr. Summers, but unfortunately, everyone can't go in. Follow me."

Mr. Summers took a journey into depression. He didn't hear Teresa ask him if he wanted her to go with him. He didn't see the nurse as she swaddled Beauty's baby. At that very moment, his only concern was Beauty. He walked toward the gurney. The white stiff sheet was pulled up to her neck.

"Doctor! Her eyes are open!" Mr. Summer's yelled.

"I can't explain it Mr. Summers. I'll close her eyes," Dr. Kipling said as he reached toward Beauty's face.

"No! Please, just give me a minute," Mr. Summers said stopping the doctor from reaching towards Beauty's eyes.

The doctor nodded and left the surgery room. Mr. Summers looked into his daughter's eyes. He felt a cold gust of wind. For a moment, he thought it was Beauty passing by with her Breeze of love. He kneeled down and cried. He looked up toward his daughter and visualized her giving him thumbs up. He smiled and raised his right thumb.

"I love you, Beauty. Daddy will always love you."

EPILOGUE

So there you have it. I was in a coma, pregnant with Randy's baby. Randy was a love like no other. Yes, we fought, but I loved him. He captured the very veins of my heart and tangled them with desires of passion. Teresa was a true friend. I could count on her to be there for me. She told the truth and said Randy was bad news from the start. It's too late to listen to her wise words now. Sarai, my next-door neighbor, was truly a diamond in the rough. Even though she lived a fast life on the streets, she had a second chance at life. I'm proud of her, even though I didn't get a chance to tell her. Kate, my best friend at work - I'll miss our Taco Tuesdays and Margarita Fridays.

I didn't get a chance to tell Aunt Elizabeth how she helped me spiritually. I wished I had another opportunity to go to church with her. Oh, and I can't forget Ms. Valley. I wanted to travel all across the world and visit the beautiful places she told me about, especially Sandals Resort in the Bahamas.

Hanging out at Joi's was my foundation. There, I was happy in my own solitude. I was Floetic Mystress. Never take life for granted. Enjoy your days while you can. Lastly, I'll miss watching Breeze on television every day. He was the boyfriend I always wanted, but never had. Too bad I'll never get a chance to meet him in person. To my darling beautiful baby boy—I hope my dad will take good care of you. Well, time is of the essence. REMEMBER, DON'T CRY FOR LOVE . . . as love always has a way of finding herself home.

Peace to all.

Don't Cry for love
Don't be afraid
Death whispers in my ear

Don't Cry for love
To my surprise
Death is truly near

Don't Cry for love
Yes one more time
I catch my lonely tears

Don't Cry for Love
I say again
The love was true my dear

Don't . . . Cry . . . for . . . Love . . .

Sincerely,
Beauty Summers

THE END